7 miles out
carol morley

BLINK
bringing you closer

Published by Blink Publishing
107-109 The Plaza,
535 Kings Road,
Chelsea Harbour,
London, SW10 0SZ

www.blinkpublishing.co.uk

facebook.com/blinkpublishing
twitter.com/blinkpublishing

978-1-910536-15-5

A CIP catalogue of this book is available from the British Library.

Design by Blink Publishing
Printed and bound by Clays Ltd, St Ives Plc

1 3 5 7 9 10 8 6 4 2

Papers used by Blink Publishing are natural, recyclable products made from wood grown in
sustainable forests. The manufacturing processes conform to the environmental regulations
of the country of origin.

Every reasonable effort has been made to trace copyright holders of material reproduced
in this book, but if any have been inadvertently overlooked the publishers would be glad to
hear from them.

Blink Publishing is an imprint of the Bonnier Publishing Group
www.bonnierpublishing.co.uk

FOR **CPC**

· STOCKPORT, ENGLAND 1977–1984 ·

last rights

It was a day not like any other. He had a new suit, for his new job, which came with a new car. I wish I could remember what make of car it was; what it looked like and what colour it was, but I can't remember any colours from that day, not one. I'm convinced that colours were different then. Not just the colour of clothes and other manufactured things but the colour of leaves, the colour of earth, the colour of skin. It's something that really gets to me, that I can't remember. It's as though I've been left with some old-fashioned, black and white movie. That kills me, it really does. No matter how much I go over that day, it's only ever in black and white.

It was summer and there wasn't much of school left to go before the holidays, but I don't remember any sunshine, not like the year before, when there had been a big heat wave. I dreamed about getting up and getting dressed, so when I did wake up for real it felt strange that I had to do it all over again. I should have taken it as a sign. I do now.

So I got dressed in my school uniform and came downstairs to find Mum carefully brushing the shoulders of his jacket with a clothes brush. I was used to him in drainpipes and as I stared at his flared trousers my mum said, 'A lady winked at him at the bus stop yesterday. Must have been his new suit.' I swear there was optimism in the air and Mum was making the most of Dad's mood, which was the sunniest it had been for a long time. While it's one of life's clichés, it did feel as though we were turning a corner. I think everyone felt it: Mum, my brother Rob, my sister Susan and even him.

Was Dad's suit brown or black? I don't think he would ever have worn navy blue. Why can't I be more precise? I'm sure that these things matter. If only I had a photographic memory, or a camera implanted in my head from birth. In fact, I used to think that after death you arrived in some big room and watched screens that replayed the whole of your life, and that if you wanted, you got to see the recordings of any other life you chose. As long as the life belonged to someone you knew. I still hope that's true, because then I could go over and over that day and colour it all in and I would be able to watch his entire life in detail. I'd give up the chance to watch my life replayed if I could watch his.

That day, Dad was about to start a new job as a sewing machine salesman and had offered to drive me to school in the new car. I sat in the front and turned and hugged the back of my seat. I was happy we had a car again. The possibilities seemed endless: pick-ups, drop-offs, day trips, visits to relatives. I remember wishing that something would happen that meant I didn't have to go to school; I had a ridiculous hope that he would ask me along for the ride to wherever he was starting work, but even though he didn't, as I clunked and clicked my seatbelt into place, a feeling of relief came over me. At least primary school was nearly over and there would be a new school to go to with the possibility of escaping Jilly and her gang. Jilly had feather-cut blond hair, soft green eyes and an elfin face. She looked so cute that nobody could have guessed at the malice that lived inside of her. Except for me. I knew. I felt the sting of her sly words and evil glances on a daily basis.

Jilly had the smallest waist of all the girls in my class. She once brought a tape measure to school and lined us up against the toilet wall and measured our vital statistics, smugly smiling when she came out the winner. I'm glad she never measured our calves, as mine were way too big for my size and I knew it. For reasons I was entirely in the dark about, apart from my calves, Jilly hated me. But I didn't hate her. I wanted to be her. I sometimes wonder now if this was exactly why she disliked me so much. I was too cringingly willing to be liked by her and too eager to stand in her shoes.

Driving along the main road, I asked Dad if he would give me a lift in the mornings when I started at my new school. He didn't answer straight away. He adjusted his rear-view mirror, thought for a while and then he just said, 'Maybe.' Over the years I've spent a lot of time on that *maybe*. It's amazing how much you can read into one little word. Had he already planned it? Or did *maybe* mean he hadn't totally made up his mind? Was there something I could have done or said to make him stay? Maybe…

If only I could remember his smell or the exact way he talked. I imagine that his smell was made up of Brylcreem because he was always smoothing his hair back with that white slick. I once bought a tub of it just to try and smell him again, but it didn't work. I couldn't trace him to the insides of that red and white tub. I know he had a Kentish accent (Kent – known as the Garden of England, he said – though he never told me why and I'm still not sure) but that's as far as it gets, I can't get his voice back into my head.

Dad didn't like the way I spoke; all the flat As and missing Gs at the end of words, and everything else that came out of my mouth that sounded Stockport and Northern. I tried hard to lose my accent in front of him, but I couldn't keep up the effort of talking differently at home and at school, so I slipped a lot. Now, seeing as I don't have to worry about school any more, I'm trying to lose my accent and talk properly, just like Dad would have wanted me to.

He parked the car outside the sweet shop, pulled on the handbrake and left the engine on. I wanted to stay in the car forever so I could avoid having to put up with all that clichéd bullying stuff I mentioned earlier, which I'm sure must have existed ever since some sadist invented schools. But even so, how come that kind of thing manages to fester and rot your soul without any adults noticing?

He came back to the car with a pack of cigarettes that he had already opened and a folded newspaper that he placed carefully on the back seat. I imagined him later at home, deep in thought, tackling the crossword puzzle. When I was much smaller I once begged him to read me a clue, which he did. He was astounded when I got the answer right and for a moment I felt like a child prodigy. I wish I could remember the question, but I only remember the answer. *Dance*. Looking back, perhaps he was only pretending I was right. Who knows? But at the time, in that moment, it felt so good to be right in front of him.

He carefully released the handbrake and with one hand steered the car into the flow of traffic. His other hand tapped a cigarette from the packet and put it to his mouth. He lit the tip with a flick of his lighter. He inhaled and the horizontal lines on his forehead

12

relaxed and then I guess I stopped looking at him and looked out of the window, thinking about my own crap, while he was watching the road and probably thinking about his. I wished I had looked at him the whole time and taken in every detail. I should have told him about all the bad things that were going on at school. What if telling him had convinced him he had a reason to stay?

But I didn't know. There was no warning that this was the last time I would ever lay eyes on him. I had no idea as we travelled along Banks Lane and drove by the boarded-up, derelict houses surrounding my junior school, that this was *it*, that he wouldn't be around to know what the world would become. What I would become.

I wanted him to wear his seatbelt that day, but he never wore his seatbelt, and it wouldn't have saved him anyway, so that's one thing I can't regret. There is something I do regret though. When he dropped me off he leant over to kiss me, but I hated being kissed back then. So I turned my head and his kiss landed in my hair. If I could change only one moment it would be that.

When I got out of the car he said, 'Do you have everything?' And I just said, 'Yeah,' or something equally dull and not really fit for being the last thing you ever say to your father. He nodded and gave his usual brief hint of a smile and said, 'Give the door a good shove to.' He didn't say goodbye; that's a detail that's sore with me, like a scab I can't stop picking. Why didn't he say goodbye? I slammed the door shut, and sealed him in.

I stood and waved as he drove away. I watched his car turn right onto Hempshaw Lane. I watched him disappear. A few seconds of real time and he was gone for good.

Ever since then I've been looking for clues.

brynn

A flash of light, her older brother takes a photograph of the family back when she was thin and her skin was smooth. Alwyn had taken up photography but she can't remember why. Her mother would pick up his prints and write on the back, make up technical details that meant nothing to her, like F/11 and 1/250, and send them off for competitions because her mother was the one bothered about things like that. Alwyn won once. She wonders where the winning photograph has gone. She's fifteen in it, her head turned to the side. Next to her is her youngest sister, just born, another sister five years old, and another, closer to her own age. She's wearing a cotton dress, made of a particular fabric. For the life of her she can't remember the name of that fabric.

Was anyone smiling in the photograph? She doesn't think anybody was. Her brother was always behind that camera, his fingers around the lens, holding a flashgun, fully confident of what he was doing. How on earth did he know what to do? She recalls that in the picture everyone else was looking straight ahead, but her gaze was in the direction of the door.

She had dreamed back then of the children she would have one day. She would put lemon in their hair and pick dandelions with them and talk about the fairies. She imagined how they would press their hot sticky little hands into hers and hold the strong hand of the husband she would one day meet who would become their father.

It seems so long ago when she met him. She was eighteen and he was nineteen. She thought he was like Elvis Presley. She hadn't been able to eat after they'd met and she knew it was a sign. If only she'd carried on not being able to eat, but now she was plagued by those extra pounds that piled on if she just happened to look at a loaf of bread.

When they arrived, her children were different to what she expected. They didn't seem to belong to her like she thought they would. Rob, her oldest son, really did seem like a miracle when he was born and at first she felt like only she owned him. And when her second child, Susan, came three years later, they were happy to have a daughter. The third and last child, Ann, was born after Ronald's affair. They thought Ann would bring them together again, and she did – for a while.

She couldn't figure out how everything had happened. How one day she was the fifteen-year-old girl in the photograph looking sideways and the next time she looked she was nearly forty and in a twenty-year marriage, with a grown-up son, daughters of seventeen and eleven – and a husband who had gone missing again.

They had once stayed in a hotel in Russell Square in London. It was their honeymoon and they'd held hands and walked to the British Museum. As they looked at the exhibits she couldn't believe how peaceful everything was. She'd thought with a stab of excitement of their first baby growing inside her and kissed him, a long slow smooch right there in the British Museum. Ronald had kissed her right back, a bit worried at first, but then with abandon and they only stopped when a guard sternly said, 'There'll be none of that in here.'

He was the only man she'd ever been with, the only man she'd ever loved. Now she is in bed, in her unfamiliar new bedroom of the house they recently moved into, and he has gone again. She no longer feels the stings of anger she once did. This is all part of the routine. She'd married an Elvis lookalike and, even though Ronald was much the same on the outside (unlike the real Elvis, who'd gone to seed), inside he'd altered so much.

He once told her that his mother had made him take his bath at exactly the same time every week, so she encouraged him to live a bit and take a bath any time he wanted. His mother had turned him against his father. It was because of her he'd never replied to that damn letter his father had sent him, and he was never the same after that. And those family doctors he went to who said 'snap out of it' weren't a help and when they did sort something out, those hospitals he ended up going to – those awful electric shock treatments, those drugs. She can't help but think of him, somewhere in his new suit with another woman. It feels better to think of him with someone else rather than on his own.

She gives up on the idea of ever sleeping.

Getting out of bed in her roll-ons and bra, she pulls on her dress and her American Tan tights, feels them drag over her psoriasis, and suddenly remembers the name of the fabric her dress was made from in that photograph. Seersucker! Funny name. She wonders where it came from. Thinking of it reminds her of her youth, of being smooth-skinned and thin. She closes her eyes, remembering.

Her eyes open. She will never be thin again and she will never sleep. She goes downstairs with the blanket and turns on the radiogram and lies on the settee and stares at the ceiling, feeling the bass of the radio but not knowing what is being said. She didn't expect to, but she falls asleep and dreams of chasing Ronald along the Margate seafront. She wakes up with an ominous shiver, her whole body shaking, and she knows. Knows that she will never catch him. A sense of relief comes over her, which seems misplaced, but nonetheless she feels it. It is the middle of the night, England is sleeping, but the thump of the foreign voices on the radiogram keeps her company. She sits up on the settee and waits.

the burial of the dead

An early knock on the door woke me up. I ran to the landing and looked down the stairs. Rob and Susan looked over the banister above me. We all waited. Mum opened the front door to a policeman and policewoman.

'Mrs Westbourne?' the policewoman said.

'No,' Mum said as she stepped backwards.

This was all we needed to see and hear to know what the news was. I knew I wasn't going to see Dad again. I knew I wasn't going to be going to school. I went back to my bedroom and pulled on my jeans and T-shirt instead of my uniform. I thought, Dad's dead and Mum's a widow, I'm not an orphan, but what am I? I rushed to the bathroom mirror and wondered if I looked like what I was, a half-orphan. I was pleased that nobody could be mean to me now. Then I felt bad for being sort of happy, what with the circumstances.

A neighbour, the mother of my sister's friend, arrived and set Rob, Susan and me to work cleaning the kitchen. We didn't talk or look at each other, and remained in our own separate worlds even though we were in the same room. I strained to catch the whispers. I was collecting evidence.

'He did it in the car.'

'A bit of hosepipe.'

'He gassed himself.'

The neighbour swung me onto her lap. I put my fists to my eyes and pretended to cry. It seemed the right thing to do. I began to concentrate on what sort of picture I made, a half-orphan on a grown-up's lap. I watched myself play the broken-hearted child. The truth was, I felt nothing at all.

'We've only got five pounds in the bank,' Mum said.

'Cremation would be a lot cheaper than burial,' the neighbour whispered over my head. Her hot breath caught on my scalp.

'I'm not wearing black. I refuse to wear black,' Mum said to nobody in particular.

*

Mum came back from the shops and held up a navy blue dress and a matching clutch bag. I thought the bag was stylish and I opened and closed the silver clasp, which gave a satisfying snap.

I don't know how I got there but I was staying at my best friend Bernice's house for a week, as I was judged too young to go to the funeral, even though I was eleven. Nobody had told me where the funeral was but I'd overheard it was near where he *did it* and it would cost less to not have to bring *the body* home.

*

Bernice told me that our teacher Mrs Finzi had announced to the class that my father had died. Knowing that everyone knew, I sat down at my school desk and sucked my cheeks in for a greater

20

half-orphan effect. I felt kind of special. I waited for the niceness of others to come my way.

But the day started like any other.

'Positions!' Mrs Finzi said.

Thirty-five of us trooped to the back of the class and lined up in dread. It was the same every morning. Mrs Finzi asked questions, one by one, and if we knew the answers we strained our hands into the air and if we were right we were allowed to sit down. The last one of us left who hadn't answered a question, Mrs Finzi labelled Dunce of the Day.

Mrs Finzi surveyed us through her half-moon lenses. Her yellow hair curled high and wide. She wore giant dangly earrings, and bright shiny dresses like tents, and she was always dabbing perfume behind her ears and on her wrists, and telling us about her dear departed Italian husband. On the rare occasions when she wasn't talking about him, she was confusing and boring us with the rules of cricket, her favourite game.

'What is the name of the river that starts here in Stockport and ends in Liverpool?' was the first question Mrs Finzi fired at us.

No hands shot up. It was news to us all that there was a river in our town. I'd never seen one. Mrs Finzi looked at us all with an expression of disbelief.

'The river Mersey of course!' she said. 'Do none of you know that the shopping centre is built over it?'

We didn't. But thinking about it, it was typical of our town to build a shopping centre over a river.

Mrs Finzi peered through the missing part of her glasses and scanned our faces, calculating her second question. 'Another name for a walk-in kitchen cupboard?'

I knew this. My Grandma Westbourne had one. I stretched my arm up and waved my hand along with everyone else, but Mrs Finzi pointed at me first with her glossy pink fingernail.

'Ann.'

I hesitated; even though I knew the answer, I was suspicious. It seemed too easy.

'A larder?'

'Correct. Be seated.'

I returned to my desk and took up looking like a half-orphan again – but then the letter came and wiped away my attempts to look like anything. It was written in misspelled capitals on yellow, black lined, paper, like it was shouting at me.

DEAR ANN, WE KNOW THAT YOURE DADS DEAD BUT NOW THAT HES DEAD WE HATE YOU EVEN MORE. YOURS SINCERELEY, JILLY AND THE GANG.

The letter punched me in the stomach and I felt sick. Even though it was against the rules to leave the class without permission, I scraped my chair back, left the letter on my desk and walked from the room into the empty corridor, which echoed with the sound of my footsteps. I hurried into the toilets and sat on a toilet seat. As horrible and strange as I felt, one thing was for sure – I wasn't going to cry. I sat there for a long time, waiting for Mrs Finzi to come and find me, but she never did. I left the toilets when the school bell rang for break, slunk to the edges of the playground and sat on a wall, my eyes to the ground, no longer caring about whether I looked like a half-orphan or not.

Bernice came over and said that the letter had been passed

around until Mrs Finzi had confiscated it and read it herself. After that she'd snatched Jilly's prefect badge away from her in front of the class, slapped her thin calves and made her stand in the corner, her back to everyone, until break.

The rest of the day is a blur of reciting times tables, spelling out words, avoiding Jilly and waiting for Mrs Finzi to say something to me, which she never did. After school I gave Bernice the slip and wandered the streets until I decided to go back to the spot where I'd last seen Dad.

I stood there and thought about how Mum had asked me on the day Dad disappeared whether he'd driven straight up the road or turned left or right after he'd left me. It seemed so important to her. If he had turned left and not right, would it have made a difference? Would he have come back to us?

Bernice and Wendy found me standing in the road.

'We've been lookin' all over,' Wendy complained.

Bernice aimed her slit-angry eyes at me. Wendy folded her fat arms and looked me up and down.

'Me mam leathered me 'cause I were supposed to look after yer,' she said.

'Soz,' I said, even though I wasn't sorry, and glad that her mum had hit her.

'I don't wanna be yer best friend any more,' Bernice said, in a matter-of-fact way.

They stood arm in arm, all cosy and full of themselves, on a mild summer night – like a photograph I wish had never been taken and that I had never seen.

I threw myself onto the road and battered my fists on the tarmac or the asphalt or whatever that rough road surface is. I don't know what I was shouting, but I was screaming something into the dust and grit of the road, and whatever it was, it was about Dad.

All I wanted was to be swallowed up into that road and vanish, but it wasn't happening, so there was nothing to do but to stand up, light-headed, dizzy and probably looking gormless. Bernice and Wendy hung in front of me like exclamation marks, gawping at me as though I was barmy. I wondered if perhaps I was. As we stood on the side of the pavement, a car turned the corner and I watched in a daze as it drove over the spot where moments before I had been sprawled out – the final place I'd ever seen Dad.

*

When Mum came back from the funeral she never mentioned anything about the ceremony to me and I had no idea what to ask, or how to go about asking. The funeral was a complete blank, another mystery to add to the list I was keeping and the clues I was trying to hunt for.

I found a letter of condolence that Mrs Finzi had written to Mum, but no matter how many times I read it, it made no mention of me; it was just from one widow to another.

The last couple of weeks of school dragged on with Jilly and her gang sending me snide looks, but nothing else. Bernice and Wendy skipped rope in unison in the playground and I made a new friend from another class. She said she didn't have any friends because she was fat and her sister was a schizophrenic. She explained in detail what schizophrenia meant and how it could creep up on you, but that you always found out if you had it properly when you were exactly seventeen. It seemed a long way off, but the thought of voices in my head preyed on my mind, and I couldn't quite shake off imagining what they would sound like if they ever did come.

on margate sands

Mum was attempting to sing *Summer Holiday* and her tuneless voice was making me cringe. Her singing trailed off and she looked at me hopefully. 'Come on, Ann.' I was never going to join in. I was not in the mood for it, and anyway, the words of the the song were about us *all* going on holiday. How could two of us make an all? We weren't all going on a holiday, we were both going on a holiday, and that just didn't have the same ring to it.

It seemed strange to be making the coach trip with just Mum. Rob and Susan were old enough and lucky enough not to have to come. Mum was wearing me out with her fake cheerfulness and I wondered how much longer I could take it. When she smiled at me I couldn't find the energy to smile back, so I spent most of the journey looking out of the window at the passing traffic.

Our annual family holiday had always been a fortnight's stay with Grandma Westbourne, Dad's mum. We never went on holiday to my mum's parents, Granddad and Granny Hughes, even though they lived near the sea too, because they didn't have the space.

Finally I glanced at Mum and saw that her face was crumpled and sad. I felt guilty, so this time I began to sing. 'There were ten in a bed and the little one said, roll over, roll over...'

Mum slowly and quietly joined in. 'So they all rolled over and one fell out...'

*

We arrived at Grandma's semi-detached house with the neatly paved front garden. As Mum knocked on the door of the house that Dad had been born and brought up in, I decided I would explore every inch of it for the clues that must be all over the place.

Grandma took ages to answer. She limped because of some never-talked-about and mysterious childhood illness, which meant she never moved very far. It was just as well, as Grandma didn't approve of people going places. She thought people should stay where God put them, that the world would be a better place for it. When she finally opened the door she was wearing a homemade flowery nylon housecoat, which wasn't a surprise, as she always wore one.

As Grandma shuffled aside to let us in, I saw the Methodist church collection box in its usual position, ready for donations. We crossed the polished wooden floor that smelt of hard work, into the back room, where we all stood awkwardly.

'So you're here,' Grandma said.

'Well, yes,' Mum said. Her face looked pinched.

Grandma's brown and grey solid waves of hair were fixed in a side parting. She never wore make-up and I realised that I had never seen her look any different. Her son had died and still she looked the same. It seemed all wrong. I wanted her to be wearing something black and to know if she'd gone to Dad's funeral. She smiled at me, a sort of half-sad smile that made me squirm.

'Looking forward to your holiday, Ann?'

'Yes, thank you.'

She put her hand in the pocket of her housecoat and pulled out ten pence and gave it to me.

'Ta, Grandma. Thank you.'

I slipped the coin into the pocket of my jeans. Grandma limped into the kitchen to put the kettle on.

The back room was the same as it had ever been. The two arm-chairs, the rug, the lampshade, the table and chairs, the small bow-fronted glass television, they were all in place and still dark brown. The coal fire that I'd never seen burning because we only ever went in the summer looked like it always did. The treadle sewing machine was in the corner, ready for action. I had hoped to see a photograph of Dad when he was a little boy, but there was not a picture of anybody anywhere in the house – apart from Jesus.

'I saw Freddie Starr was on at the Winter Gardens – I thought I'd take Ann,' Mum shouted through to the kitchen.

Grandma eventually appeared in the doorway.

'You can't take her to see that man, Brynn.' She lowered her voice. 'He tells blue jokes. It's been in the newspaper.'

Mum barked a laugh. Grandma tightened her lips.

I went outside to investigate the back garden. The runner beans were still there, climbing loyally up their sticks. Everything seemed normal: the dark green bushes, the pale pink roses, the apple tree, the patch of sheared lawn. Was this exactly how it had been when Dad was growing up? Did he eat the apples off the tree? Or string the runner beans? Maybe he even picked a rose? I tried to imagine Dad as the same age as me. I circled the garden and wished I could meet the ghost of my dad as a boy, even though I knew that was pretty much impossible; this wasn't some cosy story for children.

Through the back window I saw Mum and Grandma in the kitchen. Mum was yelling at Grandma, who was just looking at her. I decided Mum was probably shouting about Freddie Starr.

*

Mum didn't try to be cheerful as we walked to the seafront, and I tried to think of things to say to make her happy, but nothing felt right. When we got to the beach I paddled in the sea, thinking about how Dad had never finished teaching me how to swim. He once told me to put my *backside* down and I've never forgotten that he said that. It's hard to work out why some words that people say stick in your head, yet other words that are probably much more significant just vanish.

I listened to the laughter between a nearby father and son. Had Dad been taught to swim in this sea by his father? I tried to remember what Dad sounded like when he laughed, but I'm not sure he ever did – not in front of me anyway.

Mum, who I had never seen swimming, sat hunched on the towel spread out on the sand. She glanced around her before lifting the sleeves of her navy blue funeral dress, exposing her scabby skin to the sun. I had always judged her moods by her psoriasis and today it looked the worst it had ever been, like raw, flaking, miniature maps of nowhere.

*

Later on, I lay in the double bed listening to the garbled sound of

28

Mum shouting downstairs, though I never heard Grandma shouting back. Maybe it was because she was a Christian and was turning the other cheek. Christ hung on the wall opposite and I stared him out until I couldn't take his pleading eyes any more.

Mum burst in, turned the light off and got under the blankets next to me without undressing. On her side, her back to me, she sobbed and went through her own earthquake. I rested my hand on her shaking shoulder, hot and fleshy, and she talked in a tumble and I couldn't make out most of what she said but some things were clear and I stored them up. She talked about how Grandma had made Dad like he was and that she'd turned him against his own father who had upped and left when he was a boy. She said Dad had got a letter from his father asking to see him, but he hadn't gone and his father had died and soon after Dad had his first blackout. Eventually she ran out of words, and her body became cold and clammy and still.

*

In the morning when I got up, Mum pulled the pillow over her head. Downstairs, I found Grandma at her sewing machine, threading the needle with her bent, arthritic hand. Her brown eyes were magnified and cartoonish behind her glasses. I sat at the table laid for breakfast.

'Help yourself, Ann,' she said, without looking up.

Grandma clawed the dark fabric under the needle and locked it into place. Her foot pressed the treadle and the clatter began. She stopped and pulled out the joined-up pieces and cut the cotton thread with her scissors, which I was never allowed to use.

'Do you ever make men's suits, Grandma?' I asked, wondering if she had ever made clothes for my dad.

'I'm a dressmaker, not a tailor,' she snapped. She hated people getting things wrong.

I lifted the mush of milk and cornflakes into my mouth and let it dissolve and seep into the gaps between my teeth before I swallowed.

'Where's your mother?' Grandma asked.

'Still sleeping. She's not feeling very well,' I said, not wanting her to think Mum was doing something wrong by having a lie-in.

Grandma burst into a new seam. A shaft of sunlight showed up stray grey hairs trying to escape her head. Mum had said that Grandma had made Dad like he was. I concentrated on hating her, as I tried to figure out how exactly she had made Dad like he was.

She never called her neighbours by their first names, they were always Mrs This and Mr That, and they called her Mrs Westbourne. I decided that meant that nobody wanted to be her real friend. She was stingy, too. One Christmas all she sent me was some folded-up scraps of material. Had Grandma's meanness made Dad like he was?

And we were banned from the front room, arranged as a bedroom, with a single bed and a dressing table, always ready to take in a chorus girl from the Winter Gardens. 'I only take in ladies, non-smokers and abstainers. I make sure everything's above board,' Grandma often said of her lodgers, who she sometimes referred to, with a sigh, as 'dramatic theatricals'.

Had Grandma taken in 'dramatic theatricals' when Dad was growing up? I couldn't imagine it. I couldn't imagine him ever having fun with Grandma. She seemed to look down on the idea of fun. When I turned on the TV for Marc Bolan's show, she watched him sing for a few moments, winced and then said he was unsavoury and probably had nits.

Sat hunched over her sewing machine, Grandma turned around and gave me a crooked smile, the glint of a dressmaking pin held between her even, white false teeth. She pulled the silver pin from her mouth and pushed it into a miniature cushion, then took off her glasses and folded them carefully into the pocket of her housecoat. She creaked from her stool and padded over towards me in her spongy slippers. Beside me was the storage bench and she opened the lid and pulled out a silky, red dress. It was sleeveless with a drop waist and it smacked of glamour. She dangled it in front of me.

'Did yer make it, Grandma?'

'It's my wedding dress.'

As she held it against her short stout body I realised that Grandma had been thin once and, if it was possible, taller. Why hadn't she got married in white?

'It was white but I dyed it,' she said, answering my silent question. She shook with strange laughter and her eyes became glossy. I watched her uneasily. She didn't explain why she had dyed the dress red but I reckoned she did it after her husband, the grandfather I had never met, 'upped and left', as my mum had told me last night.

The door swung open and Mum came into the room, a sour smell clinging to her. Grandma stopped laughing.

'I was just showing Ann this,' Grandma said, sensible again, folding the dress back into storage.

'Were you now?' Mum said, darkly, plonking herself down at the table. She scratched her scalp and I winced as scraps of pale, thin scabs fell from her hair into my cereal bowl. I looked away, looked at the dead television, into its blank screen, and saw Mum and Grandma and me reflected there.

31

I tried to tell jokes to lift the mood, but looking back there was only one joke that I remember knowing and it was unlikely to get anyone falling off their seats. I stood in front of the fireplace and faced my glum audience.

'Where does a whale get weighed? At a whaleway station!'

*

'Well I am glad that's all over,' Mum said as she settled herself down into the coach seat before she fell asleep, her chin doubled and rested on her chest. I looked the other way, out of the window, and saw Dreamland, where we'd always gone to, year after year, and realised that even though I couldn't remember, surely Dad had some fun there – it was a funfair after all.

It was our last day, and I felt annoyed that I hadn't done much clue searching at Grandma's house and that I hadn't even found out which of the three bedrooms Dad had slept in. I was leaving behind evidence that could have helped me understand. There was one thing I had discovered from Mum's garbled talking the night before: Dad's father had left him when he was five years old, and I knew that meant something. I vowed that on the next visit I would comb every inch of space as though I was a magnifying glass.

*

But I never did go back to the house, or see Grandma again, though she kept in touch after we left. She sent us money-off coupons neatly clipped out from magazines and newspapers. Fifty pence postal orders arrived on birthdays and at Christmas, and she wrote occasional letters, written neatly in navy blue fountain pen. She mostly wrote about the price of cabbage and other vegetables, and her church duties. In the last letter Grandma Westbourne sent, four years after our final visit, she said the horses in the field nearby were behaving strangely and it must be a sign of something. She died a few days after writing that. She cut Mum out of her will and left my brother, my sister and me a letter each, to be opened and read on the day that we were married.

I'd always known her as Grandma and my mum had always called her Mum. I'd never known her first name. It's not nice, I suppose, but I didn't much care that she was dead. I was only bothered about the things that she knew about Dad that were now impossible for me to ever find out.

brynn

She remembers how he became flushed, reading the letter he got that day, and how he was shirty with her afterwards. He wouldn't tell her what was in the letter, but she found it later in the dustbin, the thin paper screwed into a ball inside the mismatched envelope. She'd smoothed it out and looked at the faint handwriting, and realised it was from Ronald's father, who he hadn't seen or heard from since he was a child.

He never did respond to the letter, and when they found out from a distant uncle that his father had died a few days later, Ronald had his first blackout, and his first breakdown came not long after that. She's always linked the death of his father and his breakdown.

She tries to imagine the letter, and at the front of her mind she maps it out, and she can almost see it, as it was; the creases in the paper, the inky words on the page, the underlined date.

Kilburn, London.

14th October 1969

Dear Ronald,

I won't go into how I got your address but I hope this letter finds you well. It is a hard letter to write but believe me when I say I have wanted to write for a long time.

I have thought about you and your sister often and I suppose you are both married with children and I am probably a grandfather.

I know that relations between me and your mother were not the best and I am sorry but please understand. It has been many years, and a lot of water under the bridge.

I am not getting any younger. I am writing to ask if I could see you. I was lately working as a Handyman, that I enjoyed, but illness has forced me to retire. My health means I am not able to travel, but I would be glad if you could visit me. I hope that you will find it in you to see me after all this time.

Yours,

Dad

under the shadow

Rob was singing into an imaginary microphone, pretending to be onstage, and his constant singing had driven my sister Susan to her boyfriend's bedsit. Mum was slumped on the settee as though she didn't want to be there at all. We had been back from Margate for two days and she hadn't even mentioned the Sex Pistols poster that had replaced the horse picture hanging over the mantelpiece.

Other things had passed Mum by as well. Rob had cut his long, fine hair into short soaped-up spikes and the back room had become the rehearsal room to Demobbed, a group my brother wasn't even in, though he had helped them get a gig once, and had been offered the job of managing them. It was odd how they had all made their way into our house during the week we were away, especially as Alby, the lead singer, hated my brother and Rob hated him. They'd apparently had some major disagreement over the music of Paul Weller and The Jam. Though I never spoke to Alby out of loyalty to Rob, who could do no wrong in my eyes, I spent the rest of the school holidays hanging out with the band.

It was Kit, the drummer, who I paid most attention to. She rimmed her eyes with kohl, had blond spiky hair and wore black, ripped T-shirts, fishnet tights and mini skirts that showed off her long thin legs that I wished were mine. Kit had run away from home and was now living with us, sleeping on a double mattress jammed in with the band's equipment in the back room, the room I imagined would be a dining room if some other family lived in the house.

Mum only realised that Kit was living with us when a vicar called at our door to persuade her to return home. I followed them into the kitchen, where Kit sat opposite the vicar and tapped out a beat on the lino with her foot. She refused to listen to his pleas for her to return to her parents and the church marching band. Mum made tea and I was pleased she appeared quite normal, seeing as she hadn't really moved from the settee for days. Our cat Tiger had been part of the family since I was tiny, and as he curled hungrily around Mum's ankles I wondered if Tiger ever thought of Dad, if he missed him, if cats could do that.

The vicar raised his shy eyes to Mum. 'We're lost without Kit, we really are,' he said. 'We worry about her.'

Mum seemed to have come out of what I had come to secretly call her widow's daze and looked like she was relishing the challenge of keeping Kit in the house, even though she hadn't noticed she was with us in the first place.

'She's as safe as one of my daughters, living here,' Mum reassured him.

He fumbled his fingers around the edge of his dog collar and gave one of those half-smiles people give when they don't really mean it. After he left, with a sad backward glance at Kit, Mum laughed. It was the first time I had heard her laugh for a long time.

So Kit continued to live with us, but, despite my full attention, which I was hoping Kit would be grateful for, she remained wrapped up in herself and she ignored me. I turned to Etta, the bass guitarist, who seemed more grateful of my company. She had chunky thighs, which she emphasised with torn-up, pale tights, wore deep-red lipstick and dyed her hair black. Etta sometimes stayed the night, but not always, though I'm not sure where she went to when she wasn't at ours – she had grown up on a farm, so it can't have been there, as there were no farms around our way as far as I knew. I think Etta liked looking for clues, like me, as she was always poking about our house, and one day I caught her coming out of the cellar.

'There's a rabbit down there,' she said. 'He looks half-starved.'

'It's Bugsy,' I said. 'I sort of forgot about him.'

She assumed he was named after Bugs Bunny. I told her he was named after the film *Bugsy Malone* but I didn't tell her it was the first and last film I'd ever gone to see with Dad, and that we'd got Bugsy soon after.

Etta said she was deeply concerned about Bugsy and took him out the front to get some air. She found a shop in the Yellow Pages that sold straw for his hutch and we both went to buy it. I loved being out on the streets with Etta. Passers-by stared at her stiletto shoes, safety-pinned tartan dress and the black cones of her hair. I wanted to parade the streets with her for as long as I could but Etta was anxious to get back to the cellar.

She held Bugsy and expertly petted his long, white ears and I pictured her on her farm, milking a cow. She offered him to me, but I was a bit scared of holding him, so she put Bugsy down to 'have a scamper' on the damp ground and set to work methodically cleaning the hutch and laying the straw. When she was finished she put Bugsy gently back inside his cage and we both bent down and peered at him through the wire grill.

'I bet he gets really pissed off in there,' I said.

It was the first time I'd sworn in front of someone that old. Etta grinned at me and I knew that a special connection had opened up between us. I made sure I got *fuck* into my next sentence.

*

My eyes adjusted as I stepped into the back room. There was enough daylight spilling around the satin-edged pink blanket hung over the window to make out the pale sheen of tangled flesh on the bed. A nipple, a thigh, something hairy, something smooth, writhing, connected. One, two, three bodies, like a human sandwich, groping and moaning: Alby, Etta and Kit. A rush of bodies rose up and re-arranged, a slash of leather whip and a muffled voice cried out. I wondered if the whip that sliced into the bodies was from Etta's farm.

Up to that point I had only thought about sex in terms of a husband and wife, a shared double bed and then a baby. I hadn't got much further than that. I was confused, but I realised that this must be sex, of a kind. Unnoticed, I stood and stared. Eventually, the writhing started to slow down and Etta detangled herself, sat up and lit a cigarette. Kit and Alby carried on pressing against each other. I was sorry for poor unwanted Etta and her thick thighs, and felt bad that she couldn't get a boyfriend of her own.

Etta inhaled on her cigarette and turned her head and saw me. She flinched for a moment before calmly exhaling a thin strand of smoke in my direction. I felt giddy and alive. An urge gripped me and I ran from the room, grabbed a pair of nail scissors from the kitchen and raced up the stairs to my bedroom, where I cut my T-shirt, making a ragged hole that exposed my stomach and belly button. A rush of pleasure that I was a punk hit me, but was quickly exchanged for guilt. What was happening in our house would not be happening if Dad had been around.

*

The holidays were nearly over and I was about to start my new school. It had been rumoured for a long time that on the first day an older pupil would force your head down a dirty toilet and flush the chain. This was one more reason that I never wanted to attend school again, but I knew that there was nothing I could do to stop it. Even when someone dies, it can only be put off for so long. Mum made further signs of emerging from her widow's daze and said she would take me shopping for a new coat and uniform. As we stepped out of the front door, I glimpsed her attempt to disguise an expression of terror and it occurred to me that she hadn't been outside for weeks.

At the market stall, I chose a red cagoule, roomy enough to last me for years. When I tried it on, Mum didn't quibble with my choice and her eyes filled with tears.

'Your daddy is looking down at you right now and he's very proud,' she said.

Why on earth would Dad be proud that I was wearing a baggy cagoule? It seemed ridiculous. Why had she gone and mentioned Dad? Why had she done that? I thought about the woman next door who screamed a lot to try and get rid of her cancer. I wanted to scream, but instead I stood there, with my head down so I didn't have to look at Mum. I stared at my shoes, thinking, let this moment be over, let all this be past.

*

School began and I joined the hundreds of other eleven-year-olds that lined the tennis courts, waiting to be put into tutor groups. Everybody was wearing dark colours and I stuck out in my red cagoule. I began to regret my choice, wondering if I would be the first new pupil to get my head put down the toilet.

Considering my cagoule, it was not a surprise when Jilly picked me out from the crowd and sauntered towards me with her feathered hair floating in the breeze, but she airily walked on by as though I no longer existed. I felt a growing sense of relief and the possibility of change. Things were going to be different.

Rushing home from school I pulled on my holey T-shirt and rejoined the revolution that was going on in our house. Susan tried hard to make things normal, and to help Mum, but she could only do so much, and spent more and more time at Greg's place, revising for her A-levels. I wished that I could have done something to make Mum feel better. Mum's regular act, to hide her constant red-rimmed eyes, was to give a weak smile and disappear into the kitchen to make tuna fish pie. Tinned tuna with a packet of Smash on top, my favourite.

*

Rob and his music had taken over our house and it felt like the whole world was on the verge of change. Not only did we have Demobbed holed up in the back room, but another band had come to stay the night on their *North West Tour*. Mum was in the bath and I was alone in the lounge watching TV when the lead singer came in. He wore black drainpipes and a white T-shirt under his navy blue jacket that looked like a school blazer, with an old-fashioned prefect badge pinned to it. His hair was dark and combed forward, making a short, uneven fringe for his flat, pale face. His unblinking eyes stared at me as he came and sat next to me. We watched *Are You Being Served?* together while he held my hand and stroked my hair. I didn't really enjoy any of this, but it seemed rude to stop him. He asked my age and told me that he was eighteen.

'So what's it like being eleven?'

I shrugged. I didn't have a clue what to say.

'What's your favourite thing to eat?' he asked.

'Tuna pie,' I said.

He seemed to find this very funny, but I wasn't sure why.

*

Next morning I stayed in bed until I heard the band leave, and then I got up. Downstairs, Mum was stretched out on the settee dozing, her funeral dress riding up her tights. I tugged her dress down and looked up and saw that the lead singer had scrawled my name and his inside a heart on the Sex Pistols poster. I grabbed the pen from the mantelpiece and I scribbled over the heart to disguise it. Thinking that I might be questioned over what it was covering, I drew similar blotches over other parts of the poster as well.

'You've gone and ruined it now,' Rob said when he saw it. I didn't say he was being unfair. I couldn't explain.

*

I stood outside Mum and Dad's bedroom door. I hadn't been in the room since Dad died and as far as I knew neither had Mum. Nowadays she slept in the lounge with the radiogram tuned in all night. I pushed the door open slightly, not wanting to let much air out in case something of Dad slipped away. I stepped inside.

The room was airless and dank and full of shadows. If a room could have a mood it was as sulky and glum as anything. When I opened the wardrobe door, I expected to see a tie or a shirt or a suit hanging there, or perhaps Dad's old table tennis trophy that was always displayed, but there was nothing of his left. It was empty.

It was the last room Dad had ever slept in, the last room he ever had dreams in, probably nightmares. I lay down on the mattress and put my face into the pillow. I inhaled, but there was not a trace of Dad.

I got under the bed and looked up at the spirals of springs. Dust and fluff drifted down into my mouth and eyes. I watched the mattress poking through from above, hoping to suddenly see the shape of a body, the shape of him. I touched a rusty spring and held my breath for as long as I could.

Perhaps none of this was real.

Maybe Dad was still alive.

I waited.

*

Marc Bolan died in a car crash, leaving a two-year-old son behind. It was his girlfriend in the driver's seat of the Mini, and even though Marc sang about driving a Rolls Royce because it was good for his voice, my brother told me that Marc couldn't actually drive. I bought a scrapbook and covered it in black sticky-back plastic and collected newspaper cuttings about Marc's accident, which Rob thought was morbid.

*

Within a few months of Dad dying, everything changed. Rob moved to London. Susan moved into a one bedroom flat with Greg. Mum got a job in the head office of a wine company. Kit, Etta and Alby's band split up and moved away. Without Etta to remind me, I kept forgetting to visit Bugsy. When I finally did go down to the cellar to see him he was dead and I took it as a sign that I was useless at looking after anything. We left that house, the last house Dad ever lived in. Later, I discovered that the man who moved in after us went mad. He took an axe to the house and chopped it up, door by door, banister by banister, bit by bit.

CRYPT

brynn

She still puts on lipstick but she doesn't know why. Everything's an effort. Even eating. She's lost weight – down to a size fourteen. She's working in an office with lots of common women who never stop talking about foreign holidays. She thinks about doing a degree. She's already got the forms. She has no qualifications, but if her son, who has a way with words, wrote the admissions essay, she would get in as a mature student. Rob and Susan – they're grown up really, but the youngest one… if it wasn't for Ann. No, shouldn't say it. But, go on, it's only a thought. If it wasn't for Ann she could just up sticks and leave. One bag packed – all you need.

She opens the handbag that she bought for his funeral and takes out the old birthday card she keeps inside. Yellow and red roses on the front, and the printed words: *A Birthday Greeting, Dear Wife*, and when she opens it a paper cut-out bouquet of roses pops up with a poem that begins: *Flowers can express so well/The things that words can't say*. She turns it over, looks at the blue ink sloping forward, the tight loops of his writing – *To My Wife, For a*

Very Happy Birthday, Darling, from your Loving Husband. Underneath he has put a mountain-heap of kisses.

She should have helped him more.

They were going to grow old together. She remembers when he first touched her and how everything came after that. His mother waited three months after Rob was born to send that card and matinée jacket. Just so she didn't have to face up to the fact that she was twelve weeks pregnant when they got married.

After the funeral, at first, she couldn't leave the house for weeks – didn't want to go outside – couldn't stop gulping and thought she would suffocate. Then one night she found herself running outside. Rob and Ann chasing her along the streets and she was screaming 'Shit' and other words, on and on, and didn't care who heard. She didn't know a four-letter word till she married him. He didn't believe it but it was true. It wasn't meant to be like this. And nobody had any idea of what she was going through. Not a clue. Piss. Fuck. Shit. The children caught her at the end of that cul-de-sac, gripped her by her arms and pulled her back to that damn house. Nowhere else to go.

She should have helped him more.

There had been good times. His fingers running through her hair, whispering her name like it was the best in the world. And his lips to hers, the kisses that made everything all right again. She longed for the boy, the man, her husband. She blamed everyone and she blamed herself. She blamed him and she never had really believed in God but she hoped he was up there in heaven and she blamed God, who couldn't possibly exist, for letting this happen.

The future gapes at her and she'll never feel ready. But she knows she has to carry on. For the sake of her children. She must go on, she will go on. She's going on.

drop, drip, drop

'We won't put Top Flat on the bell, we'll call it the Studio Flat instead, it sounds more artistic,' Mum said. 'I'm going to paint the lounge a nice shade of orange. Nice and optimistic, orange.'

Our new flat was the top floor of two houses joined together. There was a second set of stairs leading down to a mysterious, blocked-up door, which intrigued me. I often daydreamed that it was a door to another world.

Susan's boyfriend, Greg, had recently taken up photography and wanted to take my photograph in front of the ornate gates of the house nearby that we called The Mansion. He said it was an *us and them* photo, and I was the *us*. Greg had applied to go to college to study photography. He was having difficulty working out what he could do for the assignment that he'd been set for his interview.

'I've to take a photo of what a raindrop feels like when it lands,' he said, scratching his pointed chin thoughtfully. 'Not what it looks like, mind you, that would be easy, but what it *feels* like.'

*

Mickey was my first new friend at the new school. She had jet black, short, wavy hair, dark intense eyes and the most bitten-down nails I'd ever seen. Her fingers were covered in warts, which I admired and wanted to catch.

Mickey worked in the market cafe on Saturdays. The first time I visited Mickey's house she made chips like an expert. She used a sharp little knife to shave the thinnest peels and chopped the potatoes into neat, even chunks. The pan of oil sizzled on the glowing electric ring.

'Me mam won't have gas in the house,' she said. 'The last house we lived in blew up.'

She lowered the metal basket of chips into the pan. The yellow oil spluttered and spat freely into the air.

'A gasman put a note on fire sayin' do not use but it went and fell on floor. Me dad came home and never saw no note so he turned fire on. Bang! The whole house went up. It were a gas leak.'

'How come he were all right?'

'Me mam says the angels were with him that day. Sometimes she says that she wishes they hadn't been.'

'Why's that?'

''Cause he…' She trailed off.

'What?'

'Sometimes he leathers her,' she whispered. 'It's when he gets pissed. She gets on his nerves.'

Mickey lifted out the chips and tipped the basket and shared them between two plates. We drowned them in malt vinegar and shook on sparkling grains of salt. My dad had died from gas and Mickey's dad was nearly killed by gas. I felt strangely happy.

We were linked.

'Stuff that in yer gob,' Mickey said as she gave me her last chip. 'An' let's go and watch telly. Me dad's in there but he'll be off out in a mo.'

*

I decided I was going to start a secret project. Whenever I met a dad I would observe him and take mental notes. I wanted to know what other dads were up to and what I was missing. But what I really wanted was to catch a glimpse of my dad in somebody else's dad; in their gestures or expressions or their voice or looks. It was a sort of a way to get a bit of Dad back. I knew it would seem strange to everyone else in the world so I kept it quiet, but I was glad I'd thought of it.

In the lounge, Mickey knelt in front of the television, turning the dial to change the channels. Mickey's dad was sitting in his armchair staring at the TV and I began to study him for signs of 'Dadness'. I noted the dark stubble on his chin, and thought of Dad's shaving brush. I could only remember ever seeing him unshaven once, after one of his disappearing trips. I took in Mickey's dad's bloodshot eyes, his black hair that curled chaotically around his head and his moody expression, which was not the same as one of Dad's moody expressions. Mickey's dad looked up at me as he licked the edge of his cigarette paper and instead of looking away I smiled.

'D'yer want a picture or what?' he yelled.

I thought of him hitting Mickey's mum.

'Dad don't,' Mickey said. She grabbed my hand and took me upstairs to her bedroom.

We'd drawn maps of our bedrooms in Geography class and

I'd been envious of Mickey's map, which showed a dressing table, wardrobe, television and organ. Now I saw that the only things that were in Mickey's room, that in reality she shared with her brother, were two single beds placed side by side, covered with tatty blankets.

Mickey's dad was different and rougher than Dad, and I decided that was because he drank too much. When he was drunk he called Mickey's mother a 'who-er' and became violent. After a while Mickey's mum got a court order banning him from coming near her. He still kept turning up at the house so she left him for good. She took Mickey to the other side of town and moved in with her mother, Mickey's nan.

*

I made another friend at school who had a father I could study. Lucy. Everyone said she was the spitting image of Cleopatra because of her straight nose and shoulder-length black hair with a crimped fringe. She wore a badge with words so small you could only read them if you got really close: Piss Off. Lucy lived on a brand-new private housing estate where, instead of the pavements being lined with paving stones, they were made of black tarmac that got sticky when it was hot. There were no cracks in Lucy's house. There was no peeling wallpaper revealing the old layers beneath, or stairs that led to blocked-up doors. Lucy's house was new, neat and orderly, and smooth all over. Lucy's mum even set the table for breakfast the night before.

Lucy opened a drawer in her dad's bedside table and showed me a packet of condoms. I had never seen any before and studied the packaging carefully. Lucy alerted me to the use-by date, which was very old.

'It's proof,' she said. 'They've not done it for years.'

Lucy said that she'd heard children didn't like to think of their parents having sex, but that she actually wanted hers to do it. She had a portable television in her bedroom and a subscription to *Jackie* magazine, but what she really wanted was for her parents to love each other, not just be together for the sake of her.

Whenever I stayed for the weekend, Lucy's father would drive me home in his shiny company car, and Lucy would come too. He always wore a suit and tie, and, according to Lucy, he never got drunk. The only thing he liked to do that scared her was to break the speed limit. I didn't mind, but Lucy hated it and was always begging him to slow down. He always did eventually, with a deep chuckle that Lucy found embarrassing. Sitting in the back seat with Lucy I would position myself so that I could view a portion of her dad's forehead in his rear-view mirror. I would frame the hairline of his greased-back, dark, short back and sides, his lined forehead, and pretend that it was my dad, not him, driving the car.

The day Lucy's dad drove me home without her, I fantasised that I was his daughter and we were going on an outing. He let me sit in the front passenger seat and I tugged and clunked my seatbelt as I watched him turn the ignition on, push down the handbrake and turn his steering wheel. I inhaled his smell of Old Spice and Vick's Nasal Inhaler. He had terrible problems with his sinuses.

He noticed a triangular iron burn on my arm and said he thought I was too young to iron, and I was pleased that he'd noticed. He stopped for petrol and came back with a Mars Bar for me. I wondered if he ever had moods, if he ever hit Lucy or her mum? For a minute I panicked that I had accepted the Mars Bar. What if he was going to drive me somewhere and rape me?

We drew up outside our flat. 'All right, duck?' he asked and I felt mean that I had believed that he could do bad things. I decided that he was the most normal dad I'd ever met and that the Mars Bar was probably a late birthday present. I had recently turned twelve after all.

*

Special music lessons became available at school. Mickey said she'd rather learn dancing than an instrument, and thought it was totally wrong that school didn't offer dance lessons. But when Lucy signed up for clarinet, I did too. Our teacher, Mr Roberts, was hidden away at the end of a warren of small, cluttered music rooms. He said he was a retired orchestra saxophonist and was married with four daughters who had all left home. He told us to call him Bob.

Bob demonstrated how to screw a clarinet together and how to moisten the sliver of reed before clamping it to the mouthpiece with the silver ligature. We followed, and put the reeds into our mouths and wetted them with our tongues as instructed. He soon had us blowing into the clarinet and getting a noise out of it.

'Now let me show you how to do the fingering,' he said.

At home I practised every day till my lips were numb and I noticed drops of spit spilling out from the bell of the clarinet and hoped that Bob would never notice that I dribbled while I played.

Bob introduced a way of improving our technique.

'Okay, Ann, if Lucy plays a note wrong I'll slap you on the bum and then you'll slap her on her bum. And if Ann plays a note wrong, Lucy, then I'll slap you and you'll slap Ann. Okay?'

We vaguely agreed but couldn't bring ourselves to look at each other. I tightened my grip on my clarinet and wished I were somewhere else.

'Let's have a little run-through,' Bob said. 'Now pretend, Ann, that you have just played a note wrong.'

He smacked Lucy.

'Go on, Lucy. Slap Ann. On the bum.'

Lucy hit me on my lower back. Bob sighed.

'Let's see if you can show the way, Ann. Lucy has just played a note wrong.'

I slapped Lucy gently in the right place. We both winced. I hoped she could see I thought it was a really weird thing to do.

'Well done girls!' Bob said.

We quickly improved.

Neither of us wanted to play a note wrong, though it was unavoidable. I'm not exactly sure why we went along with Bob and his method. When we asked a girl who attended Bob's lessons on her own if he was ever *funny* with her she looked at us blankly. We decided it must be something about the two of us – Lucy and me. So the day she was off school with a bad cold I decided that it was unlikely that Bob would do anything silly if I was by myself. To my relief, when I arrived in class, he definitely didn't seem at all interested that I was on my own. I relaxed and played the piece I had been practising for weeks. It was a blues piece, my favourite kind of style. And I played it perfectly.

When I finished, Bob clapped. I turned and smiled at him, wishing it could always be this way.

'Should I play it again?' I asked. I was eager to.

'I'm sure there's something else we could do,' he said. 'Don't you think?'

He stroked my long hair and my fingers jammed down on the cold silver keys of my clarinet and my smile slipped. Bob shrugged and grinned.

'Go on then, once more,' he said.

I played but I couldn't concentrate. I could hear Bob fumbling with something behind me. Nervous and distracted I played a section wrong. I waited for Bob to slap me. He didn't. A strange feeling came over me and I picked up my bag and clarinet case and walked out without looking back.

*

Lucy lit her cigarette with a match and inhaled it deeply into her lungs. She passed it to me.

'Make sure yer don't dew arse it.'

She was always having a go at me for making the end of her cigarette wet. I sucked in my lips to dry them out. We had been smoking for a few weeks. The first one had made me retch and I couldn't understand how anyone smoked but Dad had so I wanted to. After trying a couple of cigarettes, they didn't taste bad at all.

I took a dry, shallow drag and exhaled. 'I'm not doing clarinet any more,' I said, passing the cigarette back to her.

'Why not?'

'It's boring.'

By the way Lucy looked at me I knew she realised something. She blew a few precise smoke rings, which she had mastered quickly, unlike me, and we watched them hover in the air, impressed by their perfect roundness, a grown-up version of soap bubbles.

'Well, I'm not going neither,' Lucy said, stubbing the cigarette out, palming the short dimp to finish later.

That weekend I visited a hair salon and told the hairdresser I wanted my hair cut short and spiky. I went through a mental list of what I had learnt about other people's dads and felt a stab of disappointment that I wasn't really finding much out at all and whatever I had discovered wasn't leading me to understand Dad. Long lengths of my hair fell to the floor and I thought of how Samson had lost all his strength when his hair was cut, but not me. I was better off without it. My mind began to wander, and I ended up thinking about Greg's photography project and about what a raindrop would feel like when it hit the ground.

moment's surrender

'If yer ever want to find me stepdad, just try looking in bookies or pub,' Helen moaned.

Helen was the only other punk at my school, so it made sense we should be friends. Waxy pale, with white hair and colourless eyelashes and eyebrows, she had a white rat called Captain that she kept in a cage at the end of her bed. He was compensation for being an only child and for her Real Dad not living with her. Real Dad would occasionally drop in unannounced. He smuggled us into the pictures to see X-rated films and we'd sit on the back row and I was always conscious of his leg against mine and his hand drifting towards my knee.

'My dad fancies you,' Helen said, matter of factly. She didn't seem bothered. I thought about being fancied by other people's dads and felt a bit sick. I pressed it to the bottom of my mind.

Helen drew her curtains against the night sky and stood at the end of her bed, showing me how Captain could run along her arm.

The more I saw Captain and Helen together, the more they resembled each other, down to the sharp angles of their top front teeth.

'Rats need touching,' Helen said, stroking Captain. 'He goes dead sad if he ain't petted.'

'Do rats live for a long time?' I asked.

'Years if yer stroke them enough.'

I took off my new patent leather, pink stilettos. Mum had sent me out to buy sensible school shoes but I'd bought the stilettos instead. I had been afraid of her reaction, but she only tilted her head back and laughed when she saw them. It was like nothing got to her any more. She never reacted how she was supposed to.

My back to Helen, I pulled off my silver-threaded black jumper, and quickly replaced it with a nightie that Helen had given me. I turned around and pulled out my chewing gum like elastic, stretching it to test how far it could go. Helen looked me up and down.

'Me mam says she used to have a figure like yours,' she said.

It hadn't occurred to me that I had a figure. Helen put Captain back into his cage and together we kicked down into the cool sheets of her bed. I took the gum out of my mouth and held the soggy lump in front of me.

'Stick yer chuddy on headboard,' Helen said. 'I always do.'

I thumbed it flat against the board and said my silent prayer, the same one I said every night. I prayed I would dream about Dad.

*

In the morning I woke up to the dull thought that I had slept through the night without dreams. Helen was already awake next to me with Captain under her nightdress.

'Did yer have any dreams?' I asked.

'Yeah,' she said. 'Captain was stuck up a dead tall tree, but I managed to fly up an' rescue him.'

'I didn't dream at all,' I said, feeling cheated.

'Me dad says that if yer don't dream then you're dead. He says that we have dreams every night but they don't stay with us.'

Had I been dreaming of Dad all this time? I turned to the headboard to retrieve my gum. It wasn't there.

'It's gone and fell into yer hair,' Helen said, laughing.

She put Captain away and tried to pick out the gum, but when that failed she used a hairdryer to try and melt it out. The heat spread the gum and it stuck to even more hair. Helen got a pair of scissors and cut a patch of gummy hair down to the roots. She held a hand mirror to the back of my head and another mirror in front and I saw the puddle shapes of baldness. I liked it. It was punk.

*

'So you've bothered to come back?' Mum said when I returned from Helen's house. 'Twelve years old and gadding about. It wasn't like that in my day.'

She was definitely reacting now.

She took an angry bite of the cheese sandwich clutched in her hand. Mum was usually on some kind of diet, eating Nimble or Slimcea bread, Ayds chocolates and Limmits biscuits and drinking the sharp lemon drink PLJ, but now, without even trying, the pounds had fallen away. I was happy that something good had come out of her becoming a widow and Mum was pleased that she had lost weight.

I sat down on the settee next to her and angled my head awkwardly towards the flickering television so she wouldn't see my bald patch. She hadn't been happy when I'd had my long hair cut, even though I had given her a thick lock of hair to keep, so it was unlikely she'd be happy now.

Tiger sat on the top of the telly, his favourite place. His tail swiped the television screen like a windscreen wiper and blocked our view. I wished it was a Monday or a Wednesday, when *Coronation Street* was on. It was Mum's favourite programme and I had watched it ever since I could remember. Mum once told me in front of Dad that Grandma Westbourne had been horrified when Dad moved Up North, as she assumed it was just like *Coronation Street*. Grandma thought the North was made up of gossipy women airing their dirty laundry in public. Dad had said that in his view his mother wasn't far wrong.

Mum took another snap at her sandwich.

'I'm not going back,' she said, her mouth full of soggy grey bread. 'I'm not stepping another foot in that office.'

I wondered if the reason was that her perm had gone wrong. Parts of her hair were broken off at the roots.

'The women at that place are far too common, Ann.'

Mum thought a lot of things were common: pierced ears, eating chips out of newspaper, sterilised milk, women with stringy necks, going abroad, waste paper baskets in lounges or bedrooms or bathrooms, eating in restaurants and putting support stickers for political parties in the window of your house.

Tiger's tail swept the television screen again, like a pendulum. Mum made a snuffling noise and I realised she was crying.

'You never hug me,' she said.

It was true, I never did. I thought of Helen telling me how important it was for Captain to be touched. I reached my arms around my mum. She was thinner, but still fleshy and warm, and she smelled of perm solution and talc. She leant her head heavily on my shoulder and sobbed loudly. I watched Tiger's coarse tongue clean his fur. I listened to the drone of the TV, to the sounds from another world, but still Mum's voice bled into my head. I saw flakes of her skin like snow on the brightly coloured swirls of carpet. I imagined that I was looking down into the room and saw the mother, the girl, the cat.

'I told that boss of his about the affair. He went and sacked the both of them. I don't think he ever forgave me for losing him that airline job before you were born.'

Mum stopped talking. Her watery blue eyes settled on Tiger and the television. A flicker of optimism crossed her face.

'One time when I was on the train on the way to visit your dad in the hospital, I saw some of the cast of *Coronation Street*.'

'Really?'

'Oh yes – there they were! In the carriage next to mine.'

I began to think about the kind of hospital Dad was in.

'What have you gone and done?' Mum said, noticing my bald patch.

'It just went and happened,' I told her.

'What a pair – me and you, hey?' Mum said, ruffling what was left of my hair as I shrank under her hand – not wanting to be part of a pair with her.

'Let's have some fish and chips,' she said.

Glad to get away, I grabbed her purse and headed for the chippy. I never knew that Dad had worked at an airline, and I imagined him having an affair with an air hostess. I thought of how different things could have been. I would never have been born if he'd gone off with her. Or maybe half of me would be made up of air hostess genes. The thought hurt my head and I leant against the counter, feeling the heat against my body as I tried to rid myself of thinking about Dad and this mystery woman.

Back home we ate the fish and chips straight from the newspaper with our fingers, which Mum did not classify as common if you were inside your own home.

*

What was I searching for? I didn't know. All I knew was that I was hoping to find something when I opened the doors of Mum's wardrobe. The funeral dress hung lonely and friendless. Mum only had one other dress and she was wearing it. It was orange.

In a cardboard box at the bottom of the wardrobe I found my dad's table tennis trophy. It wasn't like I remembered. It had always looked so solid and gold on the mantelpiece out of my reach, but as I held it I realised it was light and more like painted plastic. I read his name on the little black plaque on the front and then carefully put it back in the box, where I noticed my mum's funeral clutch bag. I snapped it open and found a clear plastic bag.

Inside the bag was an old-fashioned card. There were cut-out roses on the front that popped out – and on the back was written, in looped, inky handwriting *To My Wife, For a Very Happy Birthday, Darling, from your Loving Husband.* Dad's wristwatch was in the bag too. I slid my fingers along the brown, cracked-leather strap and across the dial. It had once circled his wrist. The hands were stuck at ten to two like a smile. I wound the watch up. It didn't work. I took out his silver lighter, but it wasn't real silver, it was too light. It was cold and patterned with wavy lines with a blank square for the owner's initials to be etched in. But Dad's initials weren't there. I flicked open the lid of the lighter and turned the wheel with my

64

thumb; there was a grind and a spark but no matter how much I tried I couldn't get it to flame.

In the plastic bag I discovered a lock of my long hair that I had given Mum. It felt strange that she had placed it in the bag with Dad's things. I held my hair in one hand and Dad's watch in the other and closed my eyes. I tried to think of a spell that could bring him back, but all I could think of was abracadabra. I said it, all the same, over and over. I opened my eyes and for the tiniest fraction of a second hoped he was there.

Like a lucky dip, I reached into the bag again and pulled out a stiff piece of paper – Dad's death certificate. I saw that the cause of death was Carbon Monoxide Poisoning. I repeated the words out-loud. I knew that he had gassed himself, but I never realised there was a proper name for what he had done.

Carbon Monoxide Poisoning: so many 'o's in the words. I hated those 'o's. They were like tubes for gas to travel through. The only use of carbon I knew was in carbon paper. I didn't understand how Dad could have been poisoned by carbon, but thought it must be significant that its first three letters were car.

I drew out and unfolded a large sheet of flimsy paper. It was a copy of a letter. Dad always used pale blue sheets of Basildon Bond, which I liked holding up to the light to see the fancy watermark, and I could tell, even without the watermark, that this was the same paper. I was holding a copy of the last letter he wrote. Where was the original?

Dad's clear handwriting leaned to the right.

Dear Brynn, I'm so sorry to do this to you and the kids. Why had Dad only written the letter to Mum? Why wasn't I mentioned? I was just lumped together with my brother and sister. We were just *the kids.* I had spent so much time thinking about Dad and yet he hadn't even bothered to mention me by name.

I took the letter to my bedroom. Dad had written that he hadn't felt the same since the last breakdown. I looked up breakdown in my dictionary. I scanned the page under *break* and found *breakdown: a stoppage through accident; collapse; disintegration; a vigorous and noisy Negro dance or the like; an analysis.*

I thought of Dad collapsing and disintegrating, surrounded by poison, and how odd it was that *break-down* also meant a kind of dance. I looked up *analysis* too, and found something that I liked the sound of: *the tracing of things to their source.*

I folded the letter into the pages of my dictionary against the definition of carbon: *a non-metallic element, widely diffused, occurring uncombined in diamond and graphite.* This seemed to have nothing to do with cars, but, as I looked further down the page, I came to *carbon monoxide (CO): a colourless, odourless, very poisonous gas.*

What had killed Dad was as invisible as air. It was nothing that I would ever see.

*

Two men slouched towards the off-licence. One man was the tallest I had ever seen while the other was the shortest, like two human fairground attractions.

"Scuse,' Helen called out to them. 'Could you go in offy and get us bottles of wine and sherry? It's for me mam.'

'That right?' Tall smirked. He took the pound notes Helen held out and shambled into the shop, while Short stayed outside and ogled us, through his thick, steamed-up glasses.

I crossed my eyes and looked down at the drops of rain running down my nose. Helen had been drunk twice before. 'Can't wait to get off me head again,' she said. I couldn't wait either; I was desperate to get off mine.

Tall came out of the shop and winked as he handed Helen the paper bag. 'Ta,' she said.

We ran off to find a secluded place to mix the booze. I anxiously gulped the last of the lemonade from the can we were going to use to mix and disguise my portion. I wondered whether I would be able to swallow the wine and sherry. In the past the smell of any kind of booze, even Christmas chocolate liqueurs, had made me want to retch.

We found a quiet spot near some bushes. Helen unscrewed the tops from the bottles and I held the tins steadily as she shared the mixture equally between them. She hid the near empty bottles in the bushes for us to come back to later.

Helen drank from her tin and she made it look easy. As I held mine gingerly in front of me, she nodded in encouragement. I lifted my tin closer and was hit by a vile smell of aftershave, turpentine and nail varnish remover. I doubted I could get the stuff past my lips.

'Hold yer nose, yer mard arse,' Helen said. 'Yer won't be mithered by taste.'

I pinched my nostrils with my fingers, lifted the tin, put my head back, poured and swallowed. A quick heat rose in my throat. I decided I was swigging a liquid chemical and I was part of an experiment. I took the next sip without holding my nose.

We roamed the shopping centre and I began to know what being drunk was like.

*

Curled up inside a shopping trolley, shop windows whizzing by as Helen pushed me at speed and let go of the handle. I was freefalling, spinning onto my side, clambering out of the trolley, amazed that my tin was still upright in my hand.

Sitting on a toilet forgetting why I was there. Coming out of the cubicle and the blotchy-faced attendant with too many outlines for one person. She picked up my tin to dump it.

'No!' I shouted. It didn't sound like my voice.

I lunged at the attendant and saw all of the layers of her shocked face. I got my tin back. I looked at my reflection and realised that it was me and wasn't me. Helen was right. Being off your head was great.

We re-filled our tins and then, I don't know, but a rush of wet warmth between my legs. Hadn't I gone to the toilet just now or was that ages ago?

'I've wet meself!' I shouted out to a lad.

Gadding. About. Twelve. Years. Old.

Helen?

'I've wet meself,' to anyone I met.

There's Helen. I'm trying to get on a bus. Helen is pushing me up the steps. Stumbling. Laughing. Driver won't let me on. Concerned expression. Funny, the way his face is serious.

'What's wrong with 'er?'

The driver radios for an ambulance.

'Run,' says Helen, dragging me away by the hood of my cagoule.

Get away. Get away. I am running, I'm running, all the layers of me, up Plaza steps, along Underbank, feet, breath, pounding.

'Where's me tin?'

Where's Helen? Don't know. Me. I am in a doorway. A shop doorway. A shadow. Lips. Hands. Teeth. Darkness.

I don't know.

*

My eyes opened to *Tiswas* on the TV. I tried to speak but no words came out. Helen was kneeling close to the screen, with Captain on her shoulder. She turned around and smiled. 'Yer puked on me mam's new cardigan last night,' she said.

We spent the rest of the morning watching the telly while Helen scratched away at the lovebites on my neck with a plastic comb, her tried and tested method of making them seem more like a naturally occurring rash.

brynn

She saw her daughter writing an essay for school entitled 'Loneliness'. She wonders what on earth Ann knows about that. She's always gallivanting off without a by your leave and dragging some unfortunate creature back with her. Slum kids, really.

She wonders if she could write a story too. She finds some paper and a pen and sits for a while. But she only writes one word – She – before crossing it off and writing He. She can't get any further.

She sometimes sees him in crowds. But when she catches up with him, it's never him, of course. Ann doesn't mention him and she doesn't mention him to Ann. That's the way. No photos on display to remind them. Move forward. No point moping about. Moping gets nobody anywhere.

She's got a new job at Debenhams – that newly built brown brick department store in Mersey Square – but she doesn't think she'll stay long. She saw a newspaper advert for a houseboat near Wigan and the rent was quite cheap and she thought that would be a nice way to live, gently rocking on the water.

She would have liked a bit more of her family around her. She thinks back to her brother's photograph and where they've all got to. Her sister Barb has just had a breakdown and is living back at home, even though she's twenty-seven. Proof that no woman should go on having kids in her forties, let alone her own mother. Her sister Jan has got three young kids and she's bringing them up on her own, which can't be easy. Her other sister married a bank manager and lives in a big house and she never sees her. Her brother has got his own photographic shop in Derby and is always busy. They were once all huddled together in a small house and she couldn't wait to get away and start her own life. Now they're all flung apart she suddenly longs to be back in that photograph with a different future ahead.

She realises she's moping and tries to snap out of it. She looks at herself in the mirror. She's heading for size eighteen. First thing in the morning she'll start a new diet.

something to show you

Of course, Mickey, Lucy and Helen didn't realise they were involved in my ongoing study on fathers, but they didn't need to know. I just made sure I took in whatever they said about them and made a note of it, along with any particularly interesting behaviour I observed for myself from their dads. So far: Mickey hadn't mentioned her dad lately and I never saw him around; Lucy's dad was going on more and more business trips and had moved out of the bedroom he shared with her mum and Helen's Real Dad was best avoided in case he clamped his hand on my knee again.

I liked to keep my friends separate and I was never going to form a gang – that was too complicated and merging. I hung out with Helen to get drunk, Lucy to smoke and Mickey to meet boys. Whenever Mickey saw a lad that she liked, she would fold her hands into fists so that they couldn't see her warts.

*

Mickey chucked the chip wrapper into the air and as it fluttered to the ground we wondered what to do next. She was wearing her new Northern Soul navy blue pinafore. She spun around on her laced up Monkey Boots and her long full skirt flared open into a circle and revealed her thin, caramel legs. She showed me a few new dance moves, which I tried to replicate.

'Can't dance fer toffee can yers,' she said.

That was true. It wasn't just my pencil skirt and stilettos getting in the way. I didn't have any rhythm.

'Look!' Mickey said, mid-spin, her eyes fixed into the distance. I followed her gaze and saw the lads coming our way. There were five of them, a little older than us, and the best one of them was a punk with bleached blond hair.

We waited until they were close, tossed them a bored look and walked away. They followed, like we knew that they would. We had no idea where we were going but when we saw the train station we flounced through the unmanned ticket office and onto the platform. I followed Mickey like a loyal dog as she carried on down the slope and onto the tracks.

My heels jammed into the stony gravel as I tottered to keep up. Mickey turned around and looked towards the lads, dropped her chin to her shoulder and bit her lip. I looked back and saw that they were still on the platform.

'Where yer going?' a lad shouted.

'Never yer mind,' Mickey replied.

If we carried on going forward we were going to end up in the blackness of the tunnel and I wondered if there would be rats and spiders crawling the walls.

Clatter, vibration.

'Train!' Mickey yelled.

I was sandwiched between the track and a high wall. Mickey had already made it onto the bank. I tried to haul myself up, but my arms were weak and my skirt tightly bound my legs. I couldn't make it.

A two-tone horn echoed in my head. There was no room for both the train and me on the tracks. I was going to be hit and I would die.

Perhaps it wasn't such a bad thing.

Mickey stretched her hand down to me but I refused to take it.

'Ann! Come on.'

I didn't care. I was going to die and I would see Dad on the other side.

'Fuck's sake yer moron!'

Headlights flared into view.

Then I thought of Mum having to open the door to another policeman.

I grasped Mickey's slim wrist. She yanked and I scraped up the wall and onto the bank like a caught fish.

The train passed us, lit-up carriage windows flashed by, the fast train to Crewe.

We sat amongst the thorny bushes in the damp air and caught our breath. Mickey's panting disappeared along with the sound of the train. She punched my shoulder hard and I rocked from the pain.

'What a barmcake!' she said.

I giggled and that got Mickey started. We laughed for ages and only stopped when we saw the lads were still gathered on the platform.

Mickey launched herself back onto the tracks in a single jump in her sturdy boots. I sat cautiously on the edge of the wall and turned around and lowered myself down before dropping. Mickey steadied me and turned impatiently. I hobbled behind her as we retraced our steps to the platform.

The lads were waiting and looked impressed, I reckoned.

'He's mine,' Mickey whispered to me, picking out the punk. I couldn't argue, after all, she had saved my life.

'Okay,' I said, selecting the next best-looking lad.

Mickey linked my arm so I didn't stumble through the wasteland, as we followed the lads to a derelict building, where we all sat, huddled in an old, boarded-up entrance. Pressed against Mickey and me, the lads had a spitting competition to see who could spit the furthest, and we listened to the sound of phlegm being gathered in their throats and watched it being forced into froth balls that were spat into the night air. The lads laughed and talked about us like we weren't there, of our meat holes, our fish holes, and I realised how terrified I was of what I smelt like and tightly crossed my legs. But I looked at Mickey and smiled, and she smiled back. We were glad to have boyfriends.

*

Mickey unfolded the ripped-out page from the *Manchester Evening News* and passed it to me.

Homeless Man Sleeps in Stolen Car.

I hurried through the article and then went back to the beginning and slowly read it again. Mickey's dad had been arrested for stealing a car and driving it under the influence. He said he had taken the car to sleep in, as he had been homeless since the break-up of his marriage. It even mentioned that he was the father of two children.

'No one'll work out it's yer dad,' I said.

'Yer won't go tellin'?'

'Cross me heart, I won't.'

Mickey took the page back and folded it carefully along the grooves that proved she must have looked at it over and over again. I felt relieved that my dad had never made it to the papers.

To cheer Mickey up, I lifted the lid on her record player, which had been given to her by her mum's new boyfriend – a good-looking TV salesman who was never around long enough for me to take notes. I put the needle onto our favourite track from Jilted John's album *True Love Stories*, which we had bought for the cash deposit on the empty pop bottles we'd collected. The music vibrated from the speaker and we sat on the edge of the bed and sang along to a song about discos and dancing and kisses.

We played it again and again. I hoped that the music would never stop. I was anxious about going to bed, as we usually stripped down to our bras and knickers, and I was wearing a bra that belonged to Mickey's mum. I had stolen it from the airing cupboard, as the bras that had been passed down to me didn't fit any more, and I was scared that Mickey would realise.

Mickey turned the overhead light off and stripped to her underwear and slipped under the covers. The streetlights glowed through the net curtain. The room was patterned with shadow and light. I slowly took my skirt off. Mickey stared at the faded nylon angel on the front of my knickers as I got into bed next to her, still wearing my jumper.

'When I babysat for next door I looked in bedroom and she had a drawer full of knickers,' Mickey said. 'Stuffed it were. Me nan says three pairs is enough. One to wear, one fer wash and one just in case.'

'My mum says that,' I said. It wasn't true, but I thought it sounded a good thing to say, seeing as I only had three pairs.

'I know this lad startin' on market on knicker stall. I bet he'll let us pinch a few.'

I pulled up the blanket and started to fantasise about having a lot of knickers.

'Aren't yer gonna take your top off?' Mickey asked.

'I'm cold,' I lied.

'But it's dead warm yer moron.'

Mickey flung back the blanket. I felt sick. I peeled my jumper off, taking as much time as possible.

'Take yer bra off,' she whispered.

She was taking her mother's bra back.

Under the covers I unhooked the bra and took it off and handed it to her. She flung it aside. Then she took her own bra off and tossed it across the room.

Mickey looked down at me and smiled and the stray light hit her small straight milky teeth.

'Let me see,' she said, and pulled the ancient blanket down to look. I braced myself and let her.

Thin shadows from her long eyelashes gently marked her cheeks. Why did she want to see what lay under her mother's bra? I looked down at her small swellings and was envious.

Mickey lay on her back and pulled the blanket over us and we linked arms like we always did before we drifted to sleep. I prayed that it would be the night I dreamed of Dad.

Instead I dreamed that Mickey's mother's bra was on a washing line, blowing to and fro in a fierce wind.

I woke up. The streetlights must have automatically turned off because it was dark.

'Ann,' Mickey whispered. I stopped breathing. I was lying on my front. Her hand slipped forwards, cupping the gusset of my angel knickers.

Her breath grazed my shoulder as I pretended to be asleep. She was waiting for something.

Her hand stayed still. What would happen if she knew I was awake? She hovered for a while before taking her hand away.

*

The rash appeared a few days later. I couldn't stop scratching it. Mum said it was a waste of time going to see a doctor, as they weren't fit to diagnose anything and I knew she had Dad on her mind – doctors hadn't done anything for him. When the rash got worse I sneaked to the GP's surgery without Mum knowing.

The doctor took a quick look at the red lumps on my skin and smiled.

'It's scabies. You can get it from being close to other people and old blankets. A parasite. Very contagious. A little mite under your skin.'

Was it like a worm burrowing its way to my bones? The thought made me ill.

Back at home I spread the ointment over my skin. The doctor had told me that I would need someone to help me put it on my back, but there was no way anyone was seeing me naked, especially Mum.

Even though I was sure I had caught scabies from Mickey and her old blanket, I didn't get a chance to discuss it with her. When I went back to school, our form teacher told us that Mickey had moved to the seaside town of Morecambe with her mother.

Mickey was gone.

I finished with my lad and started to go out with Mickey's boyfriend, Matt the punk.

*

Matt was the first boy to finger me and I spent the whole time hoping I didn't smell like fish. When he stopped he asked me to give him a heart on his stomach made out of lovebites. I liked the metallic taste of his blood in my mouth. Most of all I liked being his girlfriend and running my fingers through the hard shiny spikes of his bleached blond hair.

A few days later I phoned Matt and his mum answered the phone.

'I want them lovebites to stop,' she said.

A long static pause hung between us. I didn't know what to say, so I didn't say anything. Later, when I saw Matt, he said that his mum had called me gormless and that he didn't want to go out with me any more.

'Yer a bit of a slag anyway,' he said.

I decided I definitely smelt like fish as I tensed my body and fisted my hands and thought of Mickey hiding her warts. One minute she was there, and the next she was gone. Just like Dad. I thought of waving him off in his car like everything was normal. How moronic was that? I should have known something was wrong. It seemed as though he had gone missing my whole life. I had cried before when he had disappeared, but he'd always come back. That last time, the time he never did come back, I had thought everything was going to be okay. He would be back home just like the other times.

How wrong I was.

I was wrong about everything and now I was a slag.

brynn

Sitting on the edge of the bed, she peers into the wardrobe mirror. She blames having children for the state she's in. The weight clings to her no matter how little she eats. There are dark sags under her eyes, and a sharp line that connects her forehead to her nose but at least she isn't very lined for her age and the weight means she doesn't look stringy like some women.

She thinks of herself pregnant again. Her mother once said that when her own mother was about to give birth for the first time she thought the baby was going to come out of her belly button. She was shocked when the midwife told her that the baby was going to come out the same way it got in.

Maybe she has a headache coming on because she feels quite strange. She feels hot tears on her cheeks. She wonders if she should go back on the tranquillisers but can't bear the idea of the doctor. Anyway, she is nothing like her husband was. His case was a serious case.

Reading an Agatha Christie would take her mind off things. Was Miss Marple thin or fat? Margaret Rutherford played her fat, but she was sure in the book she was thin.

She could become a detective herself, though by rights Miss Marple wasn't a detective, she just seemed to be around murders a lot. What about moving to the country? Renting a little cottage and working in a library and writing a book like Agatha Christie? Maybe she could join the police force but there is probably an age limit or a height limit, and really she doesn't want to be a policewoman, though putting on the uniform every day would be quite nice.

He'd looked very handsome in his prison officer uniform when he'd worked at Parkhurst on the Isle of Wight. She wonders if working with those criminals had damaged his mind, but then again the prisoners who came to do the garden seemed very decent types really. Better than some people who'd never been in prison.

She stares at the ceiling and notices fine cracks. She may paint her bedroom blue and she'll start her diet again at the weekend.

the cruellest month

'Who knows the facts of life?' asked our Science teacher. The entire class put their hands up. Mr Green looked relieved and asked us to write what we knew in our exercise books.

I decided to divide what I wrote under the usual headings of Method, Results and Conclusion. *Method: A man and woman go to bed and the man puts his penis into the woman and releases seeds and blood. Result: the woman gets pregnant and nine months later a baby is born. Conclusion: Sex makes a baby.* I chewed the end of my Biro and looked at Woody who was next to me and writing enthusiastically. Realising that there was more to the facts of life than I realised, I sneaked a look at Woody's exercise book.

Woody had written: *The man gets excited and his penis gets bigger and thicker and longer and this is called a hard on and then he inserts it into a woman and cums and lets sperm out.* This was news to me. I had always thought that a man's penis was the same size at all times and I couldn't imagine how it could get bigger. I added it to my description, trying to suppress the image of Dad doing it with Mum and the air hostess.

Mr Green gave us back our books the following week.

'I've had some laughs I must say. A lot of you have got some very peculiar notions.'

We waited for an explanation, but none came. Mr Green handed me my book and I opened it hoping to discover more, but there was nothing added to my description and he hadn't crossed anything out either.

*

Our lessons at school were called periods, which was a word that haunted me. Lately I had put off going to the toilet for hours in case I found blood flowing uncontrollably from between my legs. The thought of it frightened me. I had first heard about periods when I was ten. The girl on toilet duty had drawn me inside a cubicle and had pointed down into the toilet. I was shocked to see blood in the bowl.

'It's got nowt to do with me,' she said.

'Was it an accident?'

'It comes out yer fanny.'

'Liar.'

'Oh shut it, it's dead true. It's no skin off my nose if yer don't believe me. It's so yer can have babies or summat.'

I prayed that my blood would never arrive. I crossed my legs and hoped for the best. But even though I tried to will my periods never to happen, they did. It was a frosty, chilly morning the day I woke up and found blood on my sheet. I had no idea where the blood came from, or why I needed it but I knew it meant I could have babies, though I wasn't sure exactly why. We hadn't looked at things like that in Science. Mr Green told us very little about our insides apart from where our hearts were. He put his hand to his chest and suggested that the boys do the same to feel it beating, but not the girls – in case they accidently touched something else close by.

I didn't want to tell Mum about the blood that had found its way out of me in the night, but I had to, I needed something to soak up the blood. She was in bed, asleep. I shook her gently awake. Her creased face sprang together in alarm.

'I've started,' I said.

She sat up and rubbed the sleep from her eyes.

'Oh, I should've thought. I've got nothing in. I'm sorry, love.'

She suggested that I fold up some toilet paper in my knickers till I got to school, which annoyed me because I could have thought of that. How could she be so unprepared? It was lucky that we weren't down to newspaper strips that day.

At school, Matron crossed her arms and listened with a bored expression to my rambling about how I was using toilet paper and it was my first period. She interrupted by handing me a thick white spongy oblong.

'Ten pence,' she said.

It seemed a bit steep and I felt such a fool that I could probably have bought one from her without wittering an explanation.

Lucy checked out my skirt from behind and promised me that you couldn't see the sanitary towel bulging out. The boys were always pinging my bra strap and I didn't want them noticing the towel, too. The idea of that made me ill.

*

It was not just Mum who had given up work, apparently. Council workers across the country took part in strikes to fight for better wages and working conditions. I watched the images on television of unburied bodies and rats crawling over rubbish mountains as the gravediggers and bin men stayed off work and fought for their rights. Sometimes we couldn't even watch TV because of all the power cuts.

The dinner ladies took strike action and pupils had to leave the school grounds during dinnertime as the teachers refused to break the strike and supervise us. If you lived far enough away you didn't have to come back in for afternoon classes, so I never did return. Not that I ever headed home. I went to Woody's house with him instead. His mum wasn't there as she had run off and left Woody and his dad, who according to Woody was always at work, so that was one dad I didn't get to study. Woody took every opportunity to study me though, and I spent the afternoons on my back on his bed, shivering with the cold and covered in goose bumps.

Woody never took his clothes off, but he stripped me of all mine. I asked him about his dad, while he was squeezing my mounds, wondering if he was checking if one was bigger than the other. I asked Woody if he was nervous that his dad would unexpectedly come back and find us, but he said his dad worked too far away for that to happen. I still hoped I would get to meet him, and give him the once-over at least. Eventually Woody told me that his mum had gone and left his dad because his dad was always picking up women. He described his dad's various girlfriends in great detail as I watched his side-parted long fringe sway over his eyes, while his hot hands explored my body like I was a relief map.

His plump lips got plumper and redder as he sucked blood from my thighs and the pools of his black pupils enlarged. I spent afternoons suspended in his bedroom, calm and still on his single bed, beneath his polystyrene sky, asking him questions. Against my skin I felt the scratch of his dark grey school trousers and the brush of his tie. I felt a gentle stirring in my flesh, an invisible something. I tried to pinpoint his smell, to break it down, but I couldn't.

What Woody did to me was our secret, or so I thought, until Norman, a boy in another class, told me he knew. I'm sure it was his revenge for the time he carved my name on his arm with a pencil sharpener blade and filled it in with Indian ink and I refused to let him kiss me. Norman said that he watched everything that Woody did to me because Woody would leave the back door unlocked so Norman could sneak in and climb the stairs to the landing. Had I ever noticed that the bedroom door was always ajar? That was because he, Norman, was always crouched behind it, watching, watching me naked.

I never went back to Woody's house after that, so I never did meet his dad and I kept thinking of how I couldn't get my name off Norman's arm. It was there forever, carved out of flesh and blood.

between two lives

Shelley was in my class but she was so quiet and plain it never occurred to me to get to know her. And then her father died so I made friends with her because she was someone else with a dead dad. I really wanted to ask Shelley questions. How long had she known her dad had cancer? Had she been at his bedside when he died? If so, what did she say to him on his deathbed? How did she feel about him not being around? I never did ask her though. If I did she would want to find out the truth about how my dad had died. But I liked hanging around with her and being part of her dadless life.

Shelley now lived with her sister in their auntie's attic and took me to visit her mum who couldn't cope with her children living with her any more. Her mum's bones jutted out through her jeans and T-shirt, and her face was flat and pallid. She had a shiny, red nose flecked with blackheads and she smelt of damp. Her lips looked as though they had been drawn on with crayon and were melting away.

Shelley's mum drank lager from various open tins that were scattered about the lounge. She kept the curtains drawn. The hanging bulb cast gloomy shadows over the armchairs that crammed the room. I doubted many people came to sit on them. The room was carpeted with so many different sample squares of carpet that my eyes hurt trying to figure out all the patterns. There was a dartboard on the back of the door, both the board and the door pinned with holes.

I sat down in the armchair next to Shelley, who gave me a sideways look and a nervous smile. Her mum clutched a lager tin to her flat chest. 'How could yer go and do that to me?' she said.

'If yer mean about Family Allowance I had to tell social worker yer was getting it,' Shelley said. 'Auntie gets it now. It's the law Mam.'

Her mum snarled and threw her tin across the room. It hit the wall and bounced off, leaving a spray of beer. She rolled a dart between her fingers. Her bloodshot eyes swam in their sockets. I was ready to run but she lowered the dart and abruptly smiled at me. Her missing front tooth made her seem like a child and less scary. She held a dart in the air.

'Let's play.'

She swung her dart at the board. It missed and sank into the glossy door. She fired another, which hit the board at a severe angle and hovered there for a few seconds before falling. On her third try she miraculously hit the bullseye. This perked her up and she drunkenly gathered a set of darts and slammed them sideways into my hand. She shouted encouragement as I threw them. Shelley took her turn and soon we were all playing happily and everything seemed almost normal. But Shelley's mum went one tin of lager too far because soon she was armed with a vast supply of union jack tailed darts that she hurled around the room.

'Sorry,' Shelley said as we each ducked behind a chair.

'One hundred and fucking eighty,' Shelley's mum screamed.

Meeting Shelley's mum made me glad that my mum hadn't turned to drink and that she often did have a job.

*

Drac was stocky and dark, and told me that in all likelihood she took after her father but she wasn't sure, as she had never seen a photograph of him. In any case, she was the total opposite of her mother, who was blond, slim and delicate. Drac was two years old when her father had walked out and she couldn't remember anything about him. Even so, she told me that one day she was going to find him and whatever he was like to live with, it was going to be a lot better than putting up with her mother's string of pathetic boyfriends. Her mum was currently going out with a man who was fitting the bathroom with tongue-and-groove pine, but taking his time about it.

When I turned thirteen, Drac gave me a present in two parts. First, she pierced my right ear. She used an ice cube to freeze my lobe and the sewing needle made a loud pop that frightened us both as it forced its way through the flesh of my ear. She wiped the blood away, took her own stud out and pushed it into my new hole. For the second part she took me into her bathroom, with the half finished tongue-and-groove, and dyed my hair black in the sink. We waited for the dye to take, but when she washed it off we discovered my hair had turned purple, which was even better in our eyes. She arranged my hair with wet soap into spikes.

At home I stroked Tiger and tried to bury the dread of waiting for Mum's reaction to my altered state when she got home from her new office job. I hoped she would react the same way she had when I bought my pink patent stilettos. Maybe the fact I only had one ear pierced would make it less common than having both ears pierced. I was wrong about that.

'You look like a prostitute,' she said.

'Prostitutes don't look like this.'

'And you'd know all about that?'

Mum sank into the settee and a faraway look came into her eyes.

'I didn't learn a four letter word till I got married,' she said.

Mum often seemed to say things that came out of nowhere. I turned the stud in my ear and she looked at me and laughed so long and hard that tears sprang from the corners of her eyes, and Tiger ran under the settee. I watched her for a while and then left her to it while I made her some tea. When I came back she had stopped laughing and eyed me cautiously from behind the waft of steam rising from the mug I handed her.

I wondered if she was going to mention my image again, but she just told me to fetch some money from her purse and go to the shop for a sliced loaf. On the way I passed Drac outside the chippy and we sat in a shop doorway while she ate her chips.

I dragged the fifty pence from my mum's purse along my lips. I liked the cold metallic feel of it. I slipped the coin into my mouth and used my tongue to rattle it against my teeth. It tasted of copper and earth. It drove away all my hunger pangs. I would try it all the time and perhaps I should tell Mum about it to help her lose weight.

'Don't go swallowin' it,' Drac said.

I snatched the coin from my mouth. 'Like I'd go and do that.'

'Wanna come back to mine?' Drac asked.

I nodded, it was something to do and I'd get Mum's loaf later.

She was on a diet, after all.

I sat between Drac and her mother on the settee in front of the telly. I wasn't watching. I was edging the coin onto my lips and distracted by thoughts of Dad who had once let me eat pie and chips out of newspaper wrapping. The coin flipped inside my mouth and I lost it. The fifty pence wedged in my throat.

Then I was on the floor, writhing, a hand clutching at my throat, my hand. I knew it was me, yet nothing seemed to belong to me. Only what I was thinking.

What a way to die.

I saw Drac and her mother, soft focus in the wet mist of forced watery eyes. They were giggling. They thought I was joking. And then a range of quick expressions overtook Drac's mum's face. She stood up.

'She's turning blue!'

I was dying. I was the closest to Dad I could be. And I hoped I would die but Drac's mum's expression was so stricken it made me laugh and at that moment the coin slipped down my throat. I sat up and recovered my breath. Drac watched me with awe.

'What do we do now?' Drac's mum asked.

'She'd better go to hospital,' said Drac.

I was disappointed I was still alive and worried about not being able to buy Mum's loaf. I hoped Drac's mum would give me some money to go and buy it. Instead she phoned my mum. I wondered if Drac's mum and mine would become friends and go to the pub together. I was desperate for Mum to have friends but whenever she did make one they never lasted long.

Drac's mum spoke to mine, who sent Susan over to pick me up from Drac's house to take me to casualty. My sister and I caught the bus to the hospital where I was X-rayed. The X-ray was shown to anyone passing. There it was, a big, blank, white, seven-sided shape, between ribs and shadowy organs that I didn't know the name of. Everyone that saw the X-ray looked at it, looked at me and laughed. I was admitted to a ward.

'Hello Miss Moneybox,' said the nurse on duty.

Annoyed, I realised that I was going to hear these comments all the time and even though I was thirteen years old they had placed me on the children's ward and had given me a horrible nightdress to wear that emphasised my giant bust.

*

The buzzing of the hospital lights kept me awake that night, so I lay in the crisp, cool bed and began to think about Granny Hughes, my mum's mother, and wondered what Dad must have been thinking on our visit to see her in hospital, about a year before Dad died. The hospital was in North Wales where Granny lived, but nowhere close to where she lived. I said the place name over and over under my breath. Denbigh. The hospital looked like a boarding school in my sister's *Bunty* magazines, where *The Four Marys* went.

Nobody had told me why Granny was in hospital and I knew it was not something to ask about, but I had expected to see her in bed on a ward with other patients. Instead, she had been in a big room where other people of all ages sat in upright chairs dressed in everyday clothes. Granny sat in a chair with a cigarette jammed in the corner of her mouth. A teasing length of ash hung from it and I anticipated the fall. Granny was a chain smoker and though she was fussy about the way she dressed, wearing charity shop smart skirt suits, I could always find a cigarette burn somewhere on her clothes.

Granny said that we'd all just missed Arthur, my granddad, who had left to get back to his work shift and that she was looking forward to getting back to waitressing and to normal. Her ash fell into a dry heap on her skirt and my attention shifted to Dad. He sat on the edge of his seat with his eyes to the floor. It was like he had an invisible dressmaker stitching the skin on his face with a needle and thread. His cheek kept twitching and his eyelid wouldn't stop flickering .

'Go get Mum some ciggies,' Mum had said to him.

Dad stood up and brushed down his trousers.

'Oh, he is a love,' Granny said.

Granny dipped her chin and fluttered her eyelashes at Dad. In a couple of wide strides he was gone from the room. Granny and Mum started to whisper so I couldn't hear. I looked around and saw a piano. I skipped over and lifted the shiny wooden lid and began to play. I had never had a lesson but I tinkled the stretch of black and white keys anyway, and imagined I was a proper pianist giving a concert. I was lost in the fantasy when a man in a white coat came over to me with a kind smile on his face. He told me that he was awfully sorry, but I needed to stop. I was disturbing the patients.

I looked around and saw a girl a few years older than my sister, in a red velvet smock dress with her wrists bandaged and her face fixed in surprise. There was a man with sideburns who looked a bit like Dad, his hands clutching the wooden arms of his chair, his knuckles white and his head rocking forward and back. Finally, I cottoned on. I was in a loony bin. Granny was mental. I went back over and perched on the wooden arm of Granny's seat and looked at her carefully for signs of madness. Granny coughed and took another suck on her cigarette. She exhaled with a sigh.

'I hate the Welsh,' Granny said.

'But you're Welsh, Granny!'

'Awful bloody people,' she said. 'I don't know why we bothered to come back.'

Mum turned the gold band of her wedding ring. Granny looked at me and put on a smile.

'I wanted to be a teacher but my father didn't do with women working. You know I was engaged to a lovely Welsh boy…'

'You hate Welsh people Granny!'

'He was different, he had beautiful blue eyes but I went and ran away anyway.'

'Not now, hey Mum.'

Granny seemed not to hear.

'I got a job as a scullery maid in Manchester and one day I was in Salford Park on my day off and this nice-looking lad cycled past. He stopped, turned around and came back and stopped in front of me.' She winked at me. 'That was your granddad.'

Granny took a long drag of her cigarette before it slipped from her fingers and fell onto her skirt.

'Be careful, for God's sake,' Mum said.

Granny calmly picked it up and used it to light another cigarette. Mum shook her head with disapproval as Granny dropped the old cigarette onto the floor and snuffed it out with the heel of her shoe.

'Don't look at me like that, Brynn,' Granny said, frowning. 'That's no way to look at your own mother.'

'Yer were saying how yer met Granddad,' I reminded her, eager to hear the rest of the story. Granny exhaled smoke from her new cigarette, and her expression softened.

'Before you knew it we were getting married. I gave the engagement ring from the Welsh boy to the cook. But the other week at work this man came in.'

I pictured Granny in Little Chef, wearing her waitress uniform, scurrying about and flirting with the male customers.

'I'd seen his car draw up and it was a Jaguar or it could have been a Rolls Royce it had one of those silver things on the bonnet, but he had this wonderful pure wool coat on and he came to the counter and he looked at me and said "Do you know the Hughes of Anglesey?" and I said, "I am one of the Hughes," and then he said, "Send my regards to Rose," and I said, "But that's me," and it turned out that he was the Welsh boy with the lovely blue eyes. The very one that I was engaged to be married to nearly forty years ago and he said to me, he said, "So come on Rose, where's my ring?" and I just couldn't believe it.'

Granny exhaled a dreamy cloud of smoke straight into Mum's face.

'Mum! Please.'

'He'd done well for himself. His own company and all that. He was so overjoyed to see me it was lovely and he bought me a big box of chocolates from behind the counter and he'd even lived in America! He'd been very happily married and he'd got three children.'

Mum sighed and Granny looked at her.

'I'm the one that should be worn out, Brynn, not you.'

Mum bit her lower lip as though she was trying not to say something. Granny looked back at me.

'His wife had passed away and…'

She smiled one of her faraway smiles.

'He wanted me back! Can you believe it? At my age! He wanted to be with me after all these years. I said to him, I said in no uncertain terms, I've been with Arthur for nearly forty years, we've had five children, I can't possibly leave him now.'

Mum looked worried as Dad reappeared, clutching two packs of Embassy. His eyes were glazed, as if he wasn't able to see anything properly, and his hand rubbed the lines on his forehead as though he had a headache.

*

Dad let Mum drive on the way home. I curled up on the back seat and breathed in the stale upholstery and pretended to go to sleep so they wouldn't know I was eavesdropping.

'Well it's a bit much the judge putting her in that place. For Christ's sake. Denbigh Asylum! Just for pinching some bars of chocolate,' Mum said.

'There's more to it than meets the eye,' Dad said, clicking his lighter.

'Don't be ridiculous,' Mum replied.

I hadn't known then that Dad had spent time in places like Granny was in. Visiting Granny must have brought it all back to him. Neither of them spoke again. At least, I think that was the case because after a while I really did drift into sleep.

*

I woke up and for a moment wondered if I had imagined Granny smoking all those cigarettes in the hospital. Had it really been allowed? Within seconds the thought passed as I was drawn into the routine of the ward.

'How often do you have bowel movements?' asked Matron.

'A few times a day,' I replied. Pleased that I knew a bowel movement had something to do with going to the toilet.

'Are you sure about that?'

'Yes.' I nodded, hoping I was normal.

She held out a curved stainless steel bowl and I caught my reflected purple spikes and the reek of disinfectant.

'When you go, go in this and give it a nurse afterwards. She'll search through it.'

I was never going to let anybody do that. It was humiliating for me and for them. Matron hurried off before I had a chance to tell her that I'd made a mistake about going a few times a day.

'How old are yer?' asked the mother of the toddler who slept opposite me.

'Thirteen,' I told her.

'You've got big tits for your age,' she said.

Like she had the right to talk to me. I hated her. It proved that everyone on the ward was not only talking about the hilarious incident of me swallowing fifty pence and my purple hair, but that they were also noticing the size of my chest.

Mum appeared in the ward and I wanted to disappear. She was wearing the funeral dress again, a tail of navy blue cotton fluttered from the hem and led to the ladder at the side of her tights. I felt awful, but I wanted her gone before she had properly arrived.

Mum sat down on the plastic chair next to my bed.

'You'll be the death of me,' she said, not unkindly.

'Sorry Mum.'

I smiled at the mother of the clubfoot boy who sat with a long sigh on the chair between my bed and her son's. Her dyed auburn hair matched her eyeshadow and lipstick. She caught Mum's eye.

'How yer doing? I'm knackered, I really am,' she said.

'I'm fine thank you very much,' Mum replied in a clipped voice, looking away.

Mum probably thought knackered was a swear word. Here was a moment when she could have made a friend, but she was snobby instead. Why did she have to see every single thing as common? I sank a little further into my pillow. I had nothing to say to Mum. I wondered what she was doing without me, but I didn't ask, and she didn't say. It was strange to see her not at home but in the world, with other people around her.

'Yer don't need to visit,' I said. 'I'm fine here. And it's two bus rides and all that.'

'Well, if you're sure,' Mum said.

*

Outside of visiting hours, Matron allowed us to get out of bed and sit around the ward. I escaped to the bathroom, happy to be on my own away from all the children. A nurse came in and sniffed the air. 'I thought yer was smokin',' she said.

'I've given up,' I told her.

She smiled. She wore foundation and powder but I could still see her scar. The scar was long and deep and ran noisily from the tip of her chin, along her cheek, to the side of her eye and to her forehead. Though I tried to pretend I hadn't noticed it, she was probably used to everyone staring.

'Every scar has a story yer know,' she said.

She glanced at the upside-down watch pinned to her chest and began to tell me hers. Her scar was to do with a boy she had arranged to meet after his Sunday football match eight years before.

'It were our first date and I got off bus and I looked across road and I saw him running about. It's a funny thing really, but I knew then and there that he were the lad for me, I really did. There were summat about him.

'I honest to God looked before I crossed that road. This car came out of nowhere. I couldn't get out of way. It hit me and I were spinning in air dead slow like slow-motion at the pictures, and I hit his bonnet and I smashed his windscreen and I don't remember nowt after that. They told me he drove off and left me on road.'

'Bastard!' I said.

'The funny thing was, the lad I were on way to meet saw an ambulance and he just knew it were me. He just knew.'

The nurse touched her scar with the tip of her finger and smiled sweetly.

'I nearly died. My dad refused to leave my side. He went and lost his job over it – they weren't very sympathetic – but he just wouldn't leave. Apparently he were in tears the whole time I were in a coma.'

'Wow,' I said. The idea of being in a coma, of being alive but kind of dead at the same time and being watched over by a distraught father, appealed to me.

'It turned out driver drove off 'cause he was on way home from some family party. His wife and daughter were in car with him.'

'Yer kidding?'

'The thing was, everyone reckoned he'd been drinking and so he didn't want to go and do a breathaliser thing. He were quite well to do if yer want to know. He turned up later at the hospital. He came to say he were sorry and offered to buy us a fur coat.'

'A fur coat?'

'No joke. I told him to go and get knotted. I told him where he could stick his blooming fur coat.'

'What happened to the lad yer were going to meet?' I asked.

'Oh,' the nurse said, giggling, 'I married him.'

*

My sister came to visit with her boyfriend and they brought me the new Gary Numan album. I had been secretly hoping that people might bring me presents.

'Ta Susan. Thanks Greg.'

'That's all right.'

I wondered if Susan still had the scar on her foot from when she had been run over by a car. The day it had happened Dad had answered the phone and I'd secretly watched as he stood in the hallway, his hand gripping the receiver tightly as his voice became suddenly hushed. After the call, he whispered urgently to Mum and they both rushed from the house. I had sat watching TV with my brother, worrying about what was going on and whether Susan was dead or alive.

It turned out a car had run over her foot when she was crossing the road to buy a Cadbury's Creme Egg. I remember the egg was always an important part of the story whenever it was told. When she came home, she lay on the settee under a blanket and her friends came over and she weakly showed off the tyre indentation on the side of her foot. One friend bought her a multi-pack of nail varnishes in the colours of the rainbow that I would have killed for. She was always getting presents of one sort or another. Bouquets of red roses often arrived for her from mystery men.

'Mum said the Truant Officer came to see her,' Susan said.

'But I'm in hospital.'

'Yeah, but Mum forgot to call the school to say.'

I thought of Mum avoiding explaining my situation and laughed.

On the eighth day of being in hospital, my daily X-ray showed the fifty pence had gone. All the white coats wondered how it was impossible to be aware of it making the journey from my body. I was relieved to be leaving the hospital, glad that I was no longer going to be the centre of every joke.

'Yer mam will never get that sliced loaf now,' said one of the nurses. I didn't bother smiling.

I would have caught the bus home on my own but it was the rule that you had to leave with a guardian. Mum came to collect me and I felt I was walking through the hospital corridors next to a stranger. She had random chats with passing nurses and doctors, and I found myself despairing that she had no idea how to have a proper conversation. She was always saying either too little or too much and always to the wrong people. I caught other people giving her a puzzled look as she spoke to them. Why couldn't she just be normal?

At home I lay on my bed and listened to Gary Numan's spacey electronic voice. I thought of madness and near-death experiences and realised that madness and death could happen at any moment and people around you might not even notice. I thought of Dad, driving the car that I could no longer remember the colour of, the car that he chose to die in. I kept returning the stylus to play one Numan track in particular:

'Here in my car
I know I've started to think
About leaving tonight
Although nothing seems right
In cars'

103

dig it up again

Margaret Thatcher was outside Downing Street after winning the general election. Her waved hairdo was rigid in the breeze that fluttered the collar of her blouse. 'I just about owe everything to my father,' she said, 'I really do. He brought me up—' Tiger lunged for the screen and his claws screeched down the thick glass telly window, obliterating all that she had to say about fathers.

'He's having one of his mad half-hours,' Mum said.

Tiger tore around the room. Every day he put time aside to chase invisible mice, but he seemed different today, more on edge. He jumped onto the settee and sprung onto Mum's fleshy upper arm and sunk his teeth and claws into her. She began to cry. She was pushing Tiger away, but he was refusing to let go.

'Help me, please!'

Realising there was only me to do something, I clasped Tiger around his soft spongy middle with my hands and pulled.

Tiger's teeth and claws tightened and Mum screamed as I yanked him away. I dropped him on the carpet before he could attack me. He threw himself at the wall and howled.

'Something's not right,' Mum said.

We ran into the hallway and shut Tiger in. His long thin wails mingled with our laughter. It felt wrong to be laughing, but we couldn't help it.

'We should phone a vet,' I said.

Still laughing, Mum hurriedly leafed through the *Yellow Pages* and rang a local surgery and made arrangements. She put the phone down.

'Five pounds they're charging. Cash not cheque. Daylight robbery in anyone's book,' she grumbled.

She rang Susan; Susan only had a communal phone in a hallway so nobody answered for a long time and we started to giggle again at the sound of Tiger's cries. Eventually Mum spoke to Susan and asked her to send her boyfriend with a cardboard box to come and collect Tiger. We sat down on the stairs in the hall and waited for Greg. I put my fingers in my ears and closed my eyes and listened to my breathing.

Greg arrived. Mum pushed him into the lounge and pulled the door shut behind him. Yowling penetrated deep into my head. It was the long, drawn-out sound of suffering, but I still couldn't stop laughing.

With a victorious expression and a bloody strip of claw mark on his face, Greg tiptoed from the lounge. He held the cardboard box high above his head so I couldn't see Tiger, but I could hear his sounds, which had become whimpers. Mum reluctantly pushed the five-pound note into Greg's pocket. I followed him down the stairs and onto the street where he broke into a jog, the box stretched out on his open arms, like an offering to the gods.

When Greg returned he was empty-handed. 'The vet said it looked like his liver exploded,' he said.

Greg shuffled about nervously for a few moments. I looked at him stonily and then sat down to watch television. I knew that Greg was looking at me, but I was not going to look at him even though I wanted to ask him where the liver was and what it looked like.

'There was nothing the vet could do,' he said.

'Where's Tiger now?' Mum asked.

'He's going to take care of him,' Greg said gravely. 'No extra fee.'

Greg left and Mum looked at me and smiled. Why was she trying to make things better? What was the point?

'It wouldn't surprise me if Greg went and pocketed that fiver,' she said, laughing. 'He probably didn't even go to the vet. He's down that pub right now, I can picture him.'

I hoped she was right. I decided Tiger had actually scrambled free of the box and was preying on neighbourhood mice. Maybe he'd make his own way home. Tiger had been around forever and I couldn't imagine life without him. Mum often despaired that he wouldn't eat anything but Whiskas, which was the most expensive variety of cat food. I thought of the way Mum would jokily Hoover up the end of Tiger's tail and how he always ended up with his fur standing on end.

For a few days I waited for Tiger to return, but he never came back and I realised he was gone. He would never again sit on the top of the TV and block our view with his tail.

My head felt heavy and solid and I wondered if I was about to cry. I hadn't cried for so long that I didn't know any more how it would feel. I wanted to find Tiger's body and open up his little red mouth and hold back his white whiskers and give him the kiss of life. I wanted to resuscitate him, my tabby cat with his wise green eyes.

In any case I was not going to let him be forgotten. I bought two tins of model aircraft paint from the newsagent and found a rock and painted it silver. In black paint I wrote *TIGER RIP* on the side. Outside, I laid the rock in front of the shrubbery that bordered our block of flats.

Because it was my first funeral I was not sure of what to do. I prayed that Tiger was at peace but still having his mad half-hours and that he had a healthy liver again and wherever he was they had Whiskas. On my recorder I played a made up tune that sounded serious and mournful.

The vet had probably burnt Tiger. It was cheaper than burial. I wished I had seen his dead body. 'Ashes to ashes, dust to dust,' I chanted over and over, thinking of fire, thinking of smoke, thinking of bodies disappearing.

*

The next day when I got in from school I opened the front door to a cloud of smoke. I found Mum in the bathroom, where she was fanning orange flames that flared from the bath. The edges of her hair were singed and her face was covered in soot.

'Mum, what yer doing?'

'I just wanted to get rid of things.'

'What things?'

'Just some documents.'

'What kind?'

'Stop being nosy, madam. It's none of your business.'

Mum twisted the bath taps on. Water gushed and killed the

flames. I joined her and we looked down at the sodden mash of black ashes. The wall by the bath was scorched. What had she been burning? If it was paper, couldn't she have ripped it up? What had she gone and destroyed that I didn't know about?

Mum was in one of her quiet moods afterwards. She sat on the settee in front of the TV and picked away at her scalp. I lay on the floor, feeling like her bodyguard, eyeing her out of the corner of my eye and making sure that she didn't get up to any more funny business. She fell asleep, her face still smeared with soot, her jaw grinding. I watched her orange dress rise and fall with each soft snore, and felt angry that Dad had left her behind. Even though she was asleep her expression remained tense, as if even her dreams were causing her problems.

brynn

It's satisfying to watch the orange flames destroy the red final notice bills and every official letter she has ever had. She thinks about the kind of women who burn their bras and decides that they have no idea. They're all flat-chested and don't know what it's like to need proper support.

She sometimes wishes she could do what he did and end it all. But she can't be a misery guts. She decides Ann needs to see a family in action. She's going to invite everyone for Christmas and show how it can be done under her roof. Mum, Dad, sister Jan and her kids, childless-sister Barb and her new boyfriend, and then, of course, her own kids – Rob in London with his girlfriend, tall and thin enough to get a modelling job somewhere abroad, and Susan and her boyfriend Greg. Ann will have a whale of a time with everyone around. Tomorrow she'll make the calls, she'll get the family together, she'll start a new leaf. She'll get the biggest turkey they've ever seen and she'll put on the best Christmas they've ever had in their whole damn lives.

Ann comes in and asks something ridiculous about why she's started a fire in the bath and her mood plummets. She wonders how easy it will really be to have Christmas here – it's only a small place. She decides that it's a bad idea and maybe the best thing to do on the whole is to forget about Christmas. It's seven months away and it's not like anybody cares – and it's already feeling like more trouble than it's worth.

the expected guests

Mum snaked silver tinsel around the flat while I wrote out Christmas cards to my classmates. The prettiest cards in the box, the ones with silver sparkle, were going to the people in my class at school that I liked and the ugliest ones, the candle and ivy cards, went to people that I didn't, but it was important that everyone got a card.

Mum had invited her mum and dad – Granny and Granddad Hughes – and my aunties and cousins for the festive season and said it would be the best time ever. I drew a map of where everyone would sleep.

'Put me in the bath,' Mum said, merrily.

Christmas Eve arrived and nearly everyone with it. I looked around, as coats were stripped off, bags were dropped and mugs of tea were handed out. Auntie Barb looked calm enough. She had a reputation for being highly strung and having a chip on her shoulder. My granny and granddad had quite recently been in a car accident, and so Granny arrived with a crutch and kept pulling slivers of windscreen glass from her face. According to her doctor these glass fragments were buried very deep and would make their way out over time.

'Lucky to be alive,' she said, patting me on the head by way of a greeting and explaining they had the crash because of Granddad's cataracts.

My brother had not appeared yet and I counted down the minutes till he did. The way I mostly kept in touch with Rob was to read the articles he wrote for *Melody Express*, where he reviewed gigs, or interviewed a lead singer or a band. Mum said that he was making a name for himself and pointed out to my youngest cousin something Rob had written. 'Doesn't he write neatly?' my cousin said, thinking Rob was responsible for the typeface.

The doorbell rang. My ten-year-old cousin Martin ran to answer and in strode Rob in an electric blue coat, which Auntie Jan stroked.

'Very London,' she said.

Everyone else began to fire questions at him as though he was a hero returning from the war. He stood tall in the middle of the lounge giving his answers as though he was being interviewed on television. I ran to my bedroom, sat on my bed and sulked.

Auntie Jan came in, waving a cigarette at me.

'What's going on?' she asked.

'Rob didn't even bother looking at me,' I said.

'Don't be daft,' she said. 'He's just had a long journey that's all.'

She glided her fingers over the tips of my dyed black spikes.

'I used to have my hair all colours. Pink it was once,' she said, recalling her days training as a hairdresser.

'Will yer teach me how to do proper backcombing?' I asked her.

'Course I will.'

I cheered up and followed her back into the lounge. A grey spiralling haze of cigarette smoke surrounded everyone. I sat cross-legged on the floor and watched Mum, Granny, my sister and aunties darting cigarettes to and from their mouths while Granddad carefully loaded up his pipe. Rob sat on a chair, one leg folded so his foot rested on the knee of his other leg. He didn't smoke and his fingers tapped a complicated rhythm on the chair arms.

'I'm going to become an anarchist, you know,' Granny told him. 'I said to my landlord, "We could talk all day about bribery and corruption, me and you." He didn't know where to put himself.'

Rob looked at me. 'All right Nip?' he asked. I wanted to ignore him like he had ignored me but I couldn't help but be pleased. He had called me Nip ever since I could remember because I was the nipper of the family. I missed stretching out on the settee next to him, top to toe. Most of all, I missed the way he was so good at calming Mum down.

*

On Christmas Day I was the first one up and the flat was cold and dark and the silence was not silent to me at all, but buzzed in my ears. I needed company. I shook my seven-year-old cousin awake.

'Father Christmas has been and gone!' I said.

We ate an entire selection box each, chocolate flaking and melting onto our nighties.

My best present was from Auntie Jan who had given me a book called A Thousand and One Things a Girl Can Do and had filled a shoebox with, amongst other things, Sellotape, glue and origami paper.

Rob had stayed with his girlfriend overnight. Her father was a butcher and Rob was due to return with a fresh turkey. Mum and

Auntie Jan waited anxiously for him to arrive, and when he turned up late, they peered inside the bag he offered and looked horrified.

'That's not a fresh turkey!' Mum said.

'It's frozen!' Auntie Jan said.

'It's just what he gave me,' Rob said.

'It'll never be ready in time,' Mum said. 'What do you expect me to do! It's all right for you, Rob, you're a vegetarian – but there's everyone else to feed!'

The problem was solved when Granny suggested running the bird under the hot tap.

'Well, it's a good job I've had the immersion heater on all hours,' Mum said.

She hauled the bird into the bath and left the hot water running over the icy, pale flesh. Auntie Barb remarked to everyone that she thought it was a disgraceful sight. She wouldn't let us forget it. She had met her ginger-bearded boyfriend through the vegan newsletter.

Mum insisted on making Christmas dinner without help and explained that the kitchen was too small for anyone else to fit into anyway. She popped into the lounge to fan her hot face that had turned strawberry.

'What must I look like! I haven't even had a sherry yet!' she laughed.

The smell of roast potatoes and turkey hung temptingly in the air.

'I'm starving,' I said.

'When your granddad was a boy, starving didn't mean hungry, it meant cold,' Granny said. 'Isn't that right, Arthur?'

Granddad didn't reply.

'His hearing aid's on the blink,' Granny explained.

116

Mum piled the plates high with turkey, pizza, stuffing, roast potatoes, mashed potatoes, sprouts and carrots, and we propped our plates on our knees or on the floor.

Crackers were pulled and snapped, spilling out paper crowns that we all slipped on with growing optimism. There were groans and titters as dumb jokes were read out loud. The television was turned down but not switched off, so it flickered cosily in the background. We were a real family. I wished we had a piano so that we could crowd around it and sing Christmas carols, even though none of us could play the piano.

Granddad asked for gravy.

Mum looked crushed. 'I've gone and forgotten to do the damn gravy,' she said.

Auntie Jan cast a furious look at Granddad.

'Dad, let Brynn sit and eat. She's been slaving away all morning.'

'What?' Granddad said.

'Let him have his gravy if he wants,' Granny said.

'It's OK. I've changed me mind,' Granddad said.

'Course you want gravy, Arthur. I'll go and make you some,' Granny shouted. She tried to lever herself off her chair with her metal crutch.

'He said to forget the gravy,' Auntie Jan said.

I looked at Auntie Barb. She hadn't uttered a word but I wondered if she was going to start screaming. She was tucking into her mashed potatoes and ignoring the commotion. It was probably because she was with her new boyfriend and, according to Mum, she would be on her best behaviour.

'Oh for Christ's sake I'll go and make some,' Mum said, jumping to her feet.

'You'll do no such thing,' Auntie Jan said, getting to hers and blocking Mum's way.

'For crying out loud,' Mum said. 'Let me go.'

Auntie Jan sat down with a heavy sigh and Mum made her way to the kitchen. I heard the kettle boil and she came back with a glass measuring jug and poured the powdery brown lumps of gravy over Granddad's food.

'That better is it?' Mum asked.

'I din't want it,' said Granddad.

'Oh for goodness sake, Arthur, don't be so ungrateful,' Granny shouted.

Auntie Barb scanned the room, darkly. She did the opposite of lighting up a room. 'Could we just have a bit of peace? Please?' she said.

All eyes settled on her. I imagined we were all thinking her comment was strange, seeing as she was the one that usually caused a fuss. She nudged her boyfriend.

'See?' she said.

'Now, now, Barbara,' Granny said.

Auntie Barb drained her glass of red wine and my stomach tensed. She was fifteen years younger than Mum and the complete opposite. Auntie Barb was slim with long, hennaed hair and was the only person in the family to have a degree, a Bachelor of Arts. She painted pictures of herself with one side of her face brown and the other side green. There was usually a spider plant or a cat somewhere in the background. I found it odd to think that she had passed an exam for her paintings.

'I din't want it,' Granddad said.

He looked bewildered. I was sorry for Granddad. When he wasn't working nights at the Hotpoint factory, he had his head under the bonnet of his Beetle, tinkering away at the rusty, old engine, trying for a quiet life. Since the accident, he didn't even have his car any more.

One time when we made what my Mum had called a flying visit, Auntie Barb had locked herself in the bathroom with a kitchen knife. I'm not sure what had caused her to do this, but Granddad had put his head in his hands and I overheard him saying quietly, 'If you're going to do it, just get on with it will yer?' It was funny that Auntie Barb, who had threatened to kill herself a few times, was still alive, and Dad, who had never screamed about doing it, had gone and really done it.

Mum waved a heaped fork of mash at Auntie Barb. 'I put butter in this!'

Auntie Barb opened her mouth and I thought, this time she is going to scream, but she never got a chance. Rob spun his Frisbee-sized pizza aimlessly across the room. It flew through the air and landed on Granddad's bald patch, flattening his paper crown and the few strands of hair he had. Strings of cheese and wet tomato paste patterned his stunned face.

'What did I tell you?' Auntie Barb said to her boyfriend, who obediently followed her as she stormed from the room.

'Barb!' said Granny, trying to get to her feet. 'Barbara, come back!'

'Don't you dare go after her,' Mum said.

Cigarettes were being lit in all directions. Mum wiped the pizza from Granddad's face with his crown. Rob tapped a beat on the arm of the chair, acting as though nothing was happening.

Granny struggled to her feet. 'I'm going to go and do myself in,' she said. She hobbled out, still wearing her red paper crown, and I doubted that she would make it down the stairs to the front door, but she did.

'Let her be,' Auntie Jan said as the door banged shut below.

'I'm going after her,' said Martin. He ripped off his crown and raced down the stairs. Mum looked pleadingly around the room, until her eyes fixed on Greg.

'Greg, go after them,' she ordered.

'Why should my boyfriend go?' Susan shouted. 'He's not even family.'

'It's okay, I'll go,' Greg said, with relief. Susan insisted on going with him.

Auntie Jan's crown floated off as she snatched up plates and whisked them away into the kitchen.

Auntie Barb flounced past, followed by her flaring red hair and her boyfriend, who carried her suitcase as well as his own. She made sure she slammed the door so hard when she left that the walls and floor of the flat shuddered.

'She's a selfish, self-centred so-and-so, that one,' said Mum, who was sitting down, peering from under her crown and contemplating the glowing tip of her cigarette.

Auntie Jan buttoned up her daughters' coats and took them to look for their brother and Granny.

Rob escaped to go and see his girlfriend.

'I don't know why I bother, I really don't,' Mum said and went to tackle the washing-up.

I was left with Granddad. He prodded his pipe with a wire cleaner and I wondered what him and Dad used to talk about, if anything. He glanced over at me but I knew that he had no idea who I was, as he couldn't see properly.

'Turn telly up would yer,' he said.

*

Boxing Day arrived and nobody seemed to have the energy to create another scene. Granny had been discovered alive and had been given a few large Martinis to calm her nerves.

Rob and Greg turned up to take Martin to see the football match.

'Can I come?' I asked.

'It's a boy thing,' Rob replied.

After they left I went back to bed and lifted the blankets over my head. I catalogued all the wrongs against me, and there were many. I never went anywhere. I never did anything. Mum hadn't got me a Christmas present. Rob didn't care about me and the proof was he'd bought me a Scalextric, and although I pretended I liked racing cars around the figure-of-eight track, I knew he hadn't thought about me when he bought it. Granny and Granddad had given me an address book that I knew only cost seventeen pence because Granny hadn't even bothered rubbing out the price in the front. And football was not just for boys. I had been to a match.

Dad once took me to see Manchester City.

And they had won as well.

Rob usually went with him, but I nagged Dad for ages to take me and eventually he did. Rob wasn't pleased that I took his place.

*

Dad held my hand and guided me through the crowds into the Maine Road stadium. His hand was firm around mine and I felt in seventh heaven to be part of his world. He even allowed me to pick where I wanted to go. I chose to stand near the front of the barrier, to be close to the pitch.

'Fucking right.'

'Fucking dead right.'

I glanced at Dad to see what he thought of the swearing but I couldn't tell; his face was set in concentration and he seemed miles away. The swearing men asked Dad a question about the game and I was proud when he gave the answer without any fuss that they'd been swearing.

Doyle, Bell, Clements, Summerbee, names were uttered into the air like they were gods. Come on City. The roar as our men ran onto the pitch. My team. Sky blue and white. The kick-off. The ball in play. Men around me talking over the game: *kick, dribble, free kick, corner, penalty, time-wasting.*

A triumphant roar as City scored, a communal wail of despair as our enemy equalised.

Dad had led me away before the game ended to avoid us getting mixed up in the crowds. Outside the walls, as Dad hurried me through the deserted turnstiles, the crowd exploded. Dad listened for a second and told me that City had scored and were last-minute winners. I jumped up and down on the spot to celebrate and to show Dad that I wasn't upset I'd missed the winning goal and that I was worthy of bringing to a football match. He had smiled and I had crossed my fingers in the hope he'd bring me to another game.

*

Under the cover of my blanket I began to wonder if my brother was still jealous that Dad had taken me and not him to that match. I realised that nobody could have got away with leaving people out and shouting and arguing at Christmas if Dad was around. I sat up and began to fold a sheet of origami paper. I tried to remember the bird that Dad had showed me. He'd told me he had learnt to make it as a boy, from a Rupert Bear annual, and I realised it was one of the few things I knew about his childhood. I creased the sheet, scoring lines, bending corners. I repeated steps and varied the folds. It had always amazed me that a piece of paper could turn into a bird that flapped its wings when you pulled the tail. But I couldn't do it. The red paper floated away from my grasp. Nausea rippled through me and I was sick over the side of the bed.

Vomiting took all of us that day, apart from Rob.

'It was that damn frozen turkey,' Mum said, cursing the fact that absent Auntie Barb and her vegan boyfriend were immune from sickness. She handed out buckets and bowls and wet dishcloths, before dashing to the kitchen sink to throw up.

*

Christmas was over. The house emptied out and Mum sank onto the settee and dwelt on where it had all gone wrong. The faint tangy odour of sick hung about until we finally discovered a dried, pale pool of it under the armchair.

heart of light

On the phone I asked Rob why he'd sent me a *Best wishes for your retirement* card for my fourteenth birthday. 'It's 'cause when I phone up you never seem to be doing anything,' he said. 'It's only a joke.'

I vowed to *do* something. What that something was I wasn't sure about. I considered tracking Mickey down in Morecambe, but didn't have a clue where to start. Both Lucy and Helen were going steady, so only had time for their boyfriends. Shelley had become less interesting to me once she stopped talking about her dad and Drac wasn't allowed out for a while because she'd been caught shoplifting. I looked around for someone else to do things with.

I settled on Debby, who I began to talk to in the dinner queue. She was in my year, but in another tutor group, and I was drawn to the dark shadows under her eyes that hinted at something interesting. She told me she liked my hair and wished that her mum would let her dye hers. She showed me the five white strands that had sprouted overnight in her thick, black wedges of hair.

'Me dad's not been same since his nervous breakdown,' Debby said. 'And neither have I.'

When I asked Debby what a nervous breakdown looked like she said that she didn't know, as she was nowhere near her dad when it happened.

'All I heard was that he started giving ten-pound notes away on street,' she said.

My dad wouldn't have done that. He never had any spare cash for one thing, and he never seemed to mix with people. Dad's behaviour had always seemed ordinary at the time. He got annoyed sometimes and shouted or lashed out with his hand, but that was like any dad. It was normal. I knew it probably wasn't normal that he sometimes never came home – his jacket missing from where it usually hung over the side of the armchair, rattling with small change. But I got used to Dad disappearing. He would be gone for days and when he came back he was quiet and he always stayed in bed for a day or two. But he never raved or raged or appeared to have a breakdown. Perhaps he did all that somewhere else. When I once told Dad that something got on my nerves, he had frowned and said solemnly that I shouldn't have nerves at my age.

'Are nerves real or are they just summat in your head?' I asked Debby.

'I think they're a bit of both,' she replied.

When Debby's dad was twenty-seven years old, a fortune-teller read his palm.

'She went and told him that summat terrible was going to happen to him when he were forty,' Debby said.

When her dad neared that age he began to feel really anxious and he ended up having his nervous breakdown.

'So was it destiny, do yer reckon? Or did he have the breakdown 'cause he were worried that summat was going to happen?' I asked.

'I don't like to think about it.'

Debby lived with her mum and dad. Even though they were divorced, her mum couldn't bear to see her ex-husband fend for himself. Although he didn't smile, he didn't look miserable. He was just a big, slow lump with a sticky-looking pink mouth peeping out from his scraggy yellow beard. It was hard to imagine him lecturing about English in a university, which was his old job.

'Will he ever recover?' I asked Debby.

She shrugged. 'He might do and then again he might not.'

'At least he's got a chance of getting better,' I said.

*

Debby asked me to go and see Heart of Light, a local Christian New Wave band who were on a tour of schools and scheduled to play at ours. At first I resisted, I didn't believe in religion, but thinking I had to *do* something so as not to appear retired, I agreed to tag along.

As well as Grandma Westbourne's Methodism that didn't seem to do Dad any good, it was the Religious Education classes at school that made me realise I didn't believe in religion. We would spend a whole class discussing whether it was acceptable for a biker Sikh to keep his turban on rather than wearing a motorcycle helmet, even though it was the law. My opinion was that if he was willing to risk his life then it was up to him. After a few lessons it seemed to me that most religions ended up leaving nothing up to anybody, they were merely a form of control. So I was not in favour of religion and I was not looking forward to seeing the band.

To prepare for the gig I put on ivory foundation and brushed my cheeks with a line of red blusher and, underneath that, a line of white powder, which was supposed to give the illusion of cheekbones, according to my recall of Lucy's *Jackie* magazine. I edged my eyes with blue kohl, with lines extending like wings to the sides, and coloured my eyebrows in matching blue. On top of this, to set it all, I used translucent powder. I put on a slit pencil skirt, stilettos and my red cagoule. I was ready for anything.

*

'They're brilliant!' Debby screamed. The music was so obvious and unoriginal I knew I should leave, but the band didn't deserve that sort of statement. I hung about at the back of the hall making sure people could see I was looking down my powdered nose at the whole stupid thing.

Debby's face shone and I knew it was mean of me to spoil her enthusiasm, but I did anyway. I arched my blue eyebrow. 'I'm sorry to break this to yer Debby, but they're really shite.'

Between terrible songs, the singer raised his arms to the ceiling.

'Jesus is the true rock star of our times,' he cried.

I grimaced and rolled my eyes. This was just a church sermon in disguise. The singer was trying to be cool but he wasn't at all. He ripped his black T-shirt off and revealed a hairless slender torso.

'In't he fit?' Debby swooned.

It was true. I had to admit he was. He was not far off looking like Bowie. His porcelain face was full of angles. He had divine cheekbones.

The heavy bass caught in my chest. It pounded my insides and I had to remind myself not to sway to the awful music. The singer carved his musical sermon into the ears of the crowd. Not mine, not my ears.

'The truth.'

'Sinners.'

'Our saviour.'

Suddenly I felt as though I was surrounded by thousands of people, which was impossible.

'Hope.'

Drum roll.

'Grace.'

Drum roll.

'The light.'

The words stabbed at me and began to make some kind of sense. But how could they? I saw Debby's expression and laughed, but felt spellbound too.

'Come and give yourself to Jesus!' the singer implored.

A woman smiled joyfully at me.

'Jesus wants you!' she said.

This wasn't happening.

'Open your heart to Jesus!'

'Come all ye sinners!'

A hand pushed me forwards. I felt light-headed and faint.

'Salvation.'

'Faith.'

'Solace.'

'Truth.'

'Children of God! Accept Jesus Christ as your saviour and be born again!'

I didn't remember fighting my way to the front, but I was there, pressed against the stage, my heart pounding in my chest. I raised my arms and reached for the singer.

'Hallelujah! Jesus is with you.'

He bent down and touched my cheek. An electric current rushed through my body. He was heaven sent.

'Jesus!' I cried. 'Jesus!'

Debby said my conversion happened so quickly she didn't see it coming but she made sure she followed and gave herself to Jesus too.

*

Every Sunday I attended church with Debby. It was not a normal church with stained glass windows and hard, wooden pews. It was a terraced house in Edgeley. According to some of the congregation, God was not impressed with what churches looked like, which made me wonder why anyone bothered to make most of them so grand.

We crammed into the knocked-through lounge and dining room. We were the youngest there. Everyone else was about twenty or even as old as thirty. We sat cross-legged on the floor and learnt new songs, accompanied by an acoustic guitar and a tambourine.

'Jesus is the saviour that I want to know
Heaven is the kingdom where I want to go
A saviour such as he, a sinner such as me
He came to save from the grave.'

Once the service finished, everybody circulated the room, smiling and hugging each other. I was disappointed that the singer from Heart of Light wasn't around. I would have liked to have hugged him for a long time. Apparently he was busy touring, according to Phil the acoustic guitar player – he did have God's work to do, after all.

If it wasn't raining after the service we all marched to the park to play Frisbee. I wondered if passers-by knew that we were a congregation of Christians but decided that they probably thought we were a big happy family instead. At least, I hoped they did.

One Sunday I got to church late as my bus had broken down.

'It was the devil himself trying to stop yer,' Phil told me.

'*He* will not drag *me* down to hell,' I replied.

'Jesus is going to use yer to spread his word,' Phil said, smiling.

I decided he was absolutely right. Even Phil, who had been a drug addict until he was saved, was capable of preaching God's word.

Under my bed was the Bible Phil had given me. I'd hidden it as I didn't want Mum knowing that I had been saved, as I thought she might start worrying about me. Every night I opened the Bible at a random page and read whatever my eyes fell upon. It seemed even tax collectors and whores could get into heaven as long as they believed in God. But could people who committed suicide get into heaven? It appeared to be a sin against God and I wasn't sure that they could. I wanted to ask Phil about it, but I found it too hard to bring the question up. I hoped Dad was not burning in some eternal flame. If only he had been saved maybe it would have made all the difference. Either he would be alive or, if he had gone and died, at least he would be in Heaven.

I decided I was going to devote the rest of my life to saving people. I wouldn't be a missionary or anything old-fashioned like that. I would be a pop star and spread Jesus' word that way. As I couldn't really sing, I wasn't sure of how I'd get to be a pop star, but I imagined if I prayed hard enough God would give me a voice, show me the path and set me tasks to accomplish my mission. So I flipped to a random Bible page, looking for a pointer from God, and read: *Love your enemies and pray for those that persecute you*. It was a sign. I vowed that I was going to save Jilly. Her yellow letter jumped into my mind again and made me shiver. Having spent three years hating and avoiding Jilly since junior school I realised that God was telling me it was time to face her. Even though I despised her with every atom of my being, I needed to forgive her.

The next day, I scoured the school grounds until I found her. She was smoking behind the bike sheds at the centre of a new gang. I was surprised that I could coordinate my legs enough to walk in her direction but the strength came because I was doing it for God. I stopped in front of her and noted that she was now the same height as me and realised I hadn't got much taller since Dad died.

She looked me up and down slowly and with a flick of her hair and a vague gesture with her hand, dismissed me and returned to her conversation.

'Jilly?'

'What the fuck. Stop mithering.'

'I'm Ann, from yer other school.'

'And?' she said.

I thought of Jesus.

'Jilly, I forgive yer.'

Her face crinkled up. 'What yer talking about?'

'I forgive yer for writin' that note.'

She stared at me blankly. Her gang closed around her. Was she about to give them a secret signal to start on me?

'What?' she said.

'That stuff yer wrote, the yellow letter!'

'Yer not still carpin' on about that are yer?'

How could she say that? I had never mentioned the note to her, not in all these years of her blanking me.

'Can I talk to yer? On yer own?' I asked.

Her gang straightened and grew a few inches.

'Anything you've got to say to me yer say to them.'

'I've come to save yer.'

'What?'

'I've come to forgive yer.'

'Are yer takin' piss?'

Jilly chucked her cigarette down and ground it dead with the sharp edge of her shoe. She didn't take her eyes off me.

'Do yer want a scrap or what?' she said.

'I forgive yer for hatin' me.'

I wondered what Jesus would do in my position. I fell to my knees. I clasped my hands together and looked up at her. Jilly's face twisted with laughter.

Closing my eyes, I remembered my lines.

'Jesus said I am the light of the world. He who follows me...'

Jilly stopped laughing and so did her gang. I opened my eyes.

'...will not walk in darkness but will have the light of light.'

'Fuck off!'

A froth of spit gathered at the centre of Jilly's mouth. She spat it down and I felt the wet warmth land on my face. Her gang smirked and hovered for guidance. When she turned her back to me, so did they. I left the spit and thought about my next move.

I stood up and wanted to grab Jilly by the hair and drag her head to my knee where I would kick it to a pulp, but I didn't. It wasn't because of Jesus and turning the other cheek, it was because I wasn't brave enough. I scuttled away, wiping the spit slowly from my cheek with my fingers. That was the moment when I decided that I was no longer going to spread the word of Jesus any more or to forgive anyone for anything.

Not Jilly for writing that letter.

Not Dad for going and doing himself in.

*

'I'm stoppin' being a Christian,' I said.

'Why?' Debby asked.

'I just haven't got it in me.'

Debby looked puzzled and a bit hurt but didn't ask me for any details. We didn't remain friends. She became more devout than ever and ended up going to a proper church.

Although I stopped believing in religion I still believed in God. He was in my head every day and it was as though he was interviewing me, though sometimes he let me interview him. From our conversations, I decided that he was not really in charge of the universe, had no influence in the death of Dad and that, while he must have created the world, he had lost control of it. The world was not in God's hands any more but it was not in the devil's hands either. While God may have invented us, we were now in charge of ourselves.

brynn

Ann always tells her that her singing voice is like Hilda Ogden from *Coronation Street*, but worse. She does have a point. When she was five she was told to stop singing the hymns in school assemblies and mime instead. Even so, she enjoys singing – though she can't for the life of her remember the words to any song. She makes them up as she goes along.

It's nearly midnight, but she starts to Hoover the lounge carpet, which is always her favourite time to sing, as the sound drowns out her voice. It's nagging at her that she can't remember who on earth identified her husband's body. Was it Rob? Or was it her? She thinks that if she'd identified him she would have known, and begins to wish that she had seen him dead, or remembered seeing him dead.

If only she had held his cold hand and told him that he should never have gone and done it. She would have kissed him and the heat of her lips could have put some life back into him – the life that she had drained away. Why couldn't she have let him go? He'd loved the Other Woman and if he'd gone to her he might still be alive. Her kids would have a father and she'd probably be on her own, but she was now anyway, so what was the difference?

But right now she decides actually she was a bloody good wife and he had no right to go and leave her to it. He didn't give a damn about anybody else. Everything was always about him and how could he throw their marriage away like that and do the unthinkable? She wants to scream, but she doesn't, she sings instead, an Elvis one. She sings on and on over the sound of the Hoover before she realises what the song is. Funnily enough, it's *Are you Lonesome Tonight?* and this time she probably did get some of the words right.

till I end my song

'It was tricky. He had a wife *and* a girlfriend,' Rob said.

My brother was visiting, as he was going to write a piece on Ian Curtis, the front man for local band Joy Division, who had just killed himself at the age of twenty-three.

'He was the same age as me,' said Rob.

Rob seemed full of life as he took giant strides along the pavement, but it occurred to me that you could never really tell who would go and do themselves in, so I eyed him cautiously. Ian Curtis took his own life on the eve of a tour of America. Surely he'd had everything to live for? I mean, he was going to America!

Rob stood still, which was a relief as I found it hard to keep up with him.

'Ian was a genius, Nip, a total genius,' he said. He deepened his voice and began to sing in a kind of a monotone about love and separation. He smiled. 'It's not been released yet but I know it'll be huge.'

I looked up at my brother and took in the vibrant certainty on his face. He knew exactly what was going to happen and where he was going. I was a million miles away from being a genius like him or Ian Curtis.

Life seemed pretty pointless.

'I was taken to see his body,' Rob said.

'Really?' I said, thinking of dead bodies, wanting to ask more but finding all the questions stuck in my throat.

'It's so I could write about it,' said Rob. 'About him.'

It seemed like the perfect time to ask Rob about everything. Questions such as: Was it because of Grandma and how she brought him up that Dad did what he did? Was Dad laid out for people to look at when he was dead? Why did Dad do it? Was it because he had had an affair? Had Rob ever seen Dad have a nervous breakdown? How come he was gone for a week before we found out? Could anyone have stopped him? What does someone look like when they're dead? But I couldn't bring myself to ask anything.

Rob stopped at the newsagent to buy Mum a local paper and I followed him inside. From behind his counter, Mr Gurnsey hung his mouth open at my newly-dyed green and orange hair.

'What does yer dad think of yer going around like that?' he asked.

Suddenly, I hated bobble-nosed Mr Gurnsey. I had to imagine I was origami paper to keep myself together. I tightened my folds and corners to stop myself coming undone. Why did it feel like Dad had died yesterday? It was three years ago. Why couldn't I get past it?

Mr Gurnsey never got his answer. I was out of the shop and walking alongside the main road with Rob. He didn't need to slow his pace so I could keep up, I wanted to run for miles, I wanted to run till I fell off the end of the earth.

'Do you still miss your dad?' Rob asked, gently.

What kind of question was that? Did I not look like I missed him? Could nobody see that I missed him every single nanosecond? All I wanted was to see Dad again. And Rob had said *your* dad. Was he only *my* dead dad? Were my brother and sister over him? I was such an idiot to be still thinking about him, and Dad would hate my hair. He wouldn't have let me do it. It would be long and brown and normal, and I would be doing homework and getting ready for tests, and Mum would not be a widow with a black, rotting heart. Everything would be better. I would be better.

In reply to Rob's question, I shrugged.

He smiled softly like he understood something. As far as I was concerned, he had no idea.

*

I knocked on Drac's door. Her mother opened it and gave me a wary look. She clearly hadn't got over me choking on the fifty pence and nearly dying in her lounge. Drac hovered behind her in the hallway.

'Ian Curtis went and killed himself,' I shouted to Drac.

Her mother frowned with exaggeration, as though I was always bringing trouble to her doorstep.

'Who is this Ian?' she asked.

'A musical genius,' I said proudly.

'That's right,' Drac added triumphantly, pushing by her to join me.

We rushed around to Drac's friend Linda's house to tell her the news. Linda lived up the road with her mother. She was an only child like Drac and her dad had recently gone off with some girl only five years older than she was. Linda swore that she would never speak to her father again.

Linda's lower lip trembled when we told her about Ian. She took us into her back garden and we stood around in the sunshine taking in the news.

'My brother said he'd a daughter, she's only about one or two,' I said.

'The poor little thing,' said Linda.

'Yeah,' said Drac.

We stayed silent for a while. It felt like this was a really important moment in history and I wanted to be part of it. We all did. Linda twisted her fair hair around her long slender fingers. Drac sucked the tip of her thumb thoughtfully. I inhaled the fresh hopeful smell of the newly-mown lawn. The grass had never seemed so green.

'My dad did it too,' I said.

Drac and Linda looked at me, shocked but impressed as well. I couldn't believe what I had told them.

'He did what Ian did?' asked Linda.

I nodded.

'Wow,' said Drac.

'Oh, Ann,' said Linda.

They draped their arms around me. We sat down on the lawn. Linda stroked my hand. 'Poor thing,' she said and looked at me sweetly with her cat-green eyes.

'Did he – how did he…?' Linda trailed off.

'Did he hang himself?' Drac asked.

'No,' I said.

'But he killed himself?' Drac asked eagerly.

'He did it with gas,' I said.

The sun shone brighter and I wondered why I had never told anyone before.

140

'I were last person in family to see him,' I said. 'He drove me to school in the car he gassed himself in.'

'Fuck!' said Drac.

'That's awful,' said Linda.

'Yer know what, though,' said Drac, 'I wished my dad'd killed himself. Then at least I'd know where he were.'

'That's horrid,' Linda said.

I looked at Drac's deep-set eyes and stubborn lips, and I thought about how she had never even known her father. At least I had known mine and Linda had known hers, and it was her choice not to see him.

What would Ian's daughter end up like? Would she try to find things out about her dad, like me? Would she search her face for signs of him? I couldn't find my dad in me, not in my eyes, my nose, my chin or anywhere else.

Linda squeezed my hand. A tear quivered down her cheek.

'Oh, Linda, don't,' I said.

'It makes me so sad that he left you,' she said.

I gawped in fascination as her tears flowed and wondered why I couldn't find it in me to cry too.

*

'It's called pitta bread,' said Linda as she placed the flat pale oval under the eye-level grill.

'Why's it called Peter?' asked Drac.

'It's p-i-t-t-a bread,' replied Linda, spelling it out.

'But why?'

'I dunno,' said Linda, annoyed that she didn't have an answer.

We watched the bread puff up to meet the heat.

'It's like a little miracle,' I said.

'That's right!' Linda said, happy again.

She took the breads from the grill, split them open and spread the yellow margarine. We stood around the cooker and ate them, margarine melting down our hands. Nothing had ever tasted so good.

When I left Linda's house, she pressed the rest of the pitta breads into my hand. 'I want you to have them,' she said, smiling.

*

Rob returned to London and I sat watching telly with Mum, who ate a stale, flat pitta bread. My euphoria from telling Linda and Drac about Dad had worn off and I felt like I had a hangover my head hurt so much. Mum's legs were bare and I could see how bad her psoriasis had become. Why had I gone mouthing off about Dad? She would have been horrified if she had known I had talked about him.

As penance for telling, I stopped going out after school and stayed in at weekends.

Listening to Joy Division took on a whole new meaning. Especially Ian's voice, which I felt drawn to in a way I never had before. He was a lad from around my way that had taken his own life. His songs took me straight to Dad and the possibility of what his emotions were like.

I often thought of Ian's daughter growing up without her father. She would never know him, but at least she would have his music. Once again, I tried to summon up Dad's voice. But it had gone. I couldn't do it. It was no longer anywhere in my head. I wished a recording of him talking existed somewhere. I had nothing of him to keep. And the thought of never hearing him again was too much. I deepened my voice and sang:

'This is the car at the edge of the road
There's nothing disturbed
All the windows are closed…'

hear the sound

'You can't loll around being morbid forever, Ann.'

Linda was at my doorstep, pleading with me to hang out with her. Her stiff cotton dress rustled and the fresh smell of soap powder wafted my way. It suddenly made me want to be by her side.

I stepped out, checked a door key was under the stone, and shut the door behind me. I linked Linda's arm and she covered my hand softly with hers and I never wanted the moment to end. We strolled aimlessly and I was relieved that she made no mention of Dad. I told her I was worried about my mum because she no longer had a job. She was sending me to cash her benefit books at the post office so she didn't have to leave the house. I was used to going to the launderette and the shops for her, but now she wasn't even step-ping outside.

'What we could do is get my mum to come to yours pretending to look for me,' Linda said. 'But she wouldn't really be looking for me.'

'So she'd end up staying and having a cup of tea or summat,' I said.

'That's right. They could start knitting together and then eventually they might go out shopping.' Linda looked hopeful.

I was a little concerned, as Linda's mum was a Christian. She might try and save my mum, and I knew Mum would hate anything like that. But at least Linda's mother was so nicely spoken that Mum couldn't possibly think she was common, which was one thing in her favour.

'I'm not even sure she'll let her in,' I explained.

'We can only give it a go,' Linda said.

Would Mum open the door? I doubted it, but just as I was feeling in a hopeless position and beginning to despair about my mother being a hermit, she unexpectedly got a new job. All plans for Linda's mum to visit mine vanished because Mum was training to be a market researcher. She was going to phone people up from an office and ask them about the adverts on the television.

Equipped with a ruler and a red pen, Mum spent her evenings going through telephone directories underlining a particular row of names and numbers, and copying them onto sheets of paper. She told me it was called random number selection and it would be used by her and the other market researchers to telephone people and ask them what they thought about the commercials. She let me help, and as the television hummed soothingly in the background and I copied out names from the directory, I imagined the people behind the names. What they looked like. What their lives were like. What they would be in the middle of doing when they answered the phone to Mum.

*

I took up smoking again for something to do. I was fourteen and getting no closer to finding out what I wanted to do with my life and, more importantly, why Dad had gone and ended his, or what a proper dad really was. Not one dad or stepdad I had met was suitable material to study for one reason or another. In fact, most of the time they were hardly around, or I was hardly around them, and that made it more difficult. I had taken to studying men with children wherever I went, watching them from a distance, trying to work out what was going on, but I wasn't really getting anywhere.

I'd run out of cigarettes, and Mum, who was what she termed a 'very occasional' smoker, didn't have any, so I rummaged around the flat, down the side of the settee and in the kitchen drawer, and found enough change to buy a packet of ten No.6 from the machine outside the sweet shop.

I traipsed to the park, sat on a bench and smoked a cigarette right down to the filter, so I felt the scorch of it on my fingers. An old lady sat down next to me and struck up a conversation. She asked me what I wanted to be when I grew up. It seemed like a sign from God that she was interested in my future. I thought very hard about what the best solution could be. I needed money to look after Mum and I needed space to figure out all the things that needed figuring out and I needed to spread the word, not of religion, but of *something*.

'A pop star.'

The lady nodded and didn't seem taken aback – another sign, I reckoned.

'Have you heard of The Hollies?' she asked.

'I think so,' I said, though I hadn't.

'My son was in them,' she said.

'Really?'

147

'They had Top 40 hits.'

Her pale blue eyes twinkled. Was she my guardian angel? God must have sent her to keep me on course. What were the chances of meeting the mother of a pop star in the park? God worked in mysterious ways. It was true.

'What does your father do?' she asked.

I was suspicious. She should have known this if she was a real angel. Then her eyes narrowed and I immediately felt under scrutiny, and that maybe she was just testing me.

'He's dead.'

'Oh. I'm sorry. How awful… He must have been young to die.'

This was true. He was a lot younger than she was.

'Do you mind if I ask how he died?'

My stomach knotted and I nearly told her the truth, then I almost told her that he died of cancer, but at the last minute changed my mind.

'In a car crash.'

'How terrible,' she said, tightening the knot of her headscarf.

It would have been so much easier if Dad had died in a crash like Marc Bolan. People could understand that. It was an accident, not a choice. But instead Dad had *wanted* to die, which was really embarrassing.

The old lady looked as though she was going to ask me something else.

'I'm sorry. Got to dash,' I said.

*

When I got home, I told Mum that I had met the mother of one of The Hollies.

'Fancy that,' she said hopefully. 'You never can tell.'

Even if she was not my angel, I wondered whether meeting the old woman was a sign that being a pop star truly was my destiny and decided that it probably was.

I put aside the reality that I couldn't sing and reminded myself that punk had proved that you didn't have to be able to sing well to be in a group, you just needed to have something to say. I wasn't sure exactly that I had anything to say but was hoping it would come to me.

My look for being in a band consisted of a purple net skirt, a faded lace cardigan and a shiny black overcoat, all bought from The Spastics Society, the best charity shop in town. I tied a strip of black net around my head and flared the net over my face like the veil on an old-fashioned pillbox hat. I wore black satin ballet shoes with leather soles, which were a bit of a hazard when it rained, but were worth it as they completed the overall impression of what I thought I should look like as a lead singer.

After perfecting my image I put an advert in the window of Rhythm Corner.

Girl singer (14 years old) – likes Joy Division/Siouxie and the Banshees/The Slits/The Raincoats/Au Pairs/Magazine/Crispy Ambulance/listening to John Peel – looking for people with own gear to form band.

Linda said she would be my number one fan and I wondered if that would mean she would let me kiss her. Thoughts of kissing her had begun to dance around in my mind. Drac wanted to be in the band but didn't want to be a backing singer and didn't have an instrument, so said that she would be a number one fan as well.

Gus and Chris joined first. They were both eighteen and worked together in a local warehouse. Gus was a big fan of David Bowie and looked quite like him, only with acne. Chris looked older than he was, as his hair was thinning on top – a family curse, he told me with a melancholic stare. He bought a drum machine for the band as he said we didn't need the hassle of a drummer, they would only throw sticks and tantrums. Perry was my age and the last to join. He had a Korg synthesiser and his shaved hair was emphasised by the long portion over his face that he referred to as his 'post-modernist fringe'.

We spent ages trying to come up with a name for our band. I had read a short story by Ray Bradbury called *The Playground*. It was about a father who was so worried about what his child would go through at school that he swapped places with his own son, exchanging his mind with his son's mind. We decided to use the title, although we carried on debating for hours over whether we should keep *The* in the title. In the end we decided that just Play-ground sounded better.

For some reason I developed an urge to see Chris and Gus kiss. When I asked them to neck in front of me they refused.

'We're not bent,' Gus said.

'We're not even bi,' added Chris.

'It's totally Bowie and Bolan,' I said.

That convinced them. They kissed while I shouted directions.

*

Linda said the youth leader at her club was a big fan of Joy Division and would let Playground rehearse at the club for free. Twice a week we practised, and Linda and Drac would sometimes come along and watch. I tried to gauge how good our songs were by their reactions. I hoped Linda was falling in love with me now that I was a lead singer, but she was so nice to everybody it was hard to tell.

A friend of a friend of the youth club leader, apparently a father of twin daughters, became our manager and we got our first gig. It was in the back room of a pub in Macclesfield, a few miles outside of Stockport. Ian Curtis came from Macclesfield, so we decided to dedicate the night to him.

'You're going to be stars!' our manager raved.

'Dead right,' I said.

There was a raised platform in the corner for our equipment. I had to imagine Linda and Drac were there, as they had to stay at home because their mums wouldn't let them come to Mac on a school night. I unfolded my music stand and rested two small dolls and the book *Amelia Jane Again* by Enid Blyton on it. Various types and ages of men holding dripping pints of beer swarmed in, grumbling about the fifty pence entry fee, and I wondered how many of them had kids at home and why none of them had brought their wives along.

Our manager gave us the thumbs up and we began. Our songs were dark and gothic, they were about vivisection and lost youth. I hoped I was going to come across as a mix of Siouxsie Sioux, Iggy Pop and Ian Curtis, not that any of the old men in the audience would have a clue who they were. I gripped my microphone and began to sing:

'And the pain in their eyes
And the fear on their breath
And the tears and the cries
As they suffer till death.'

The song ended after a frenzy of guitar. Some of the men laughed but I ignored them. One day they would be sorry. I closed my eyes and launched into the next song.

'An old woman walking down on the beach
A regular haunt in her younger days
She picks up a doll that lies discarded and torn
Look at the love in its eyes
Look at the love in its eyes.'

When we finished our set, I leant close to the microphone. My lips buzzed as a fierce feedback sliced the room.

'Thank you Macclesfield – home to the late, great Ian Curtis!' I said.

A man sidled up to me and handed me a beer mat. I was about to find a pen so I could sign my autograph when he said it was some new lyrics that he'd written for me. I turned over the mat and read: *An atom bomb is on its way / and we will end up dead today.* The man sniggered and I smiled sardonically in return.

While the others sorted out the equipment, I went to find our manager for a review of our performance. He was outside with his girlfriend. As I got closer, his girlfriend shooed me away with a wild flap of her hands, so I hung back. Our manager began to shout garbled words. I observed him with interest. Soon he was sobbing. It was the first time I had seen a grown man cry. I had never seen Dad cry, or Rob, or Granddad. Our manager stamped his feet and wailed, and I wondered if his children – his two daughters – had ever seen him this way. His eyes passed over me like he had never seen me before, and then he was sprinting up the road, followed by his girlfriend, never to be seen again.

I imagined that what I had seen was nowhere near what a nervous breakdown would look like, though I decided that people that had breakdowns did cry. I tried to think of tears running down Dad's face. Had he cried in that car before he killed himself? It was so hard to summon up tears sliding down his cheeks but I didn't really want to imagine them either. I didn't like it when people cried and I was glad that I hadn't cried since I was a kid.

We never got the five pounds or the lift home our manager had promised. Gus had to phone his dad to come and pick us up, and when his father arrived he seemed almost pleased that it hadn't gone well for Gus or the band. He told us that we'd never get anywhere if we didn't cover popular songs. All that time we'd spent over the name of the band and all the songs came to nothing. Gus left the band that night and the group ground to a halt without his guitar melodies, and never performed again.

summer nights

'Just think, me and you on holiday together,' I said to Linda. 'It'll be a right laugh!'

The youth club leader had organised a week in a holiday apartment in Devon, free of charge. Linda was upset that Drac couldn't come, as her mum and the tongue-and-groove boyfriend had made other plans, but she did think it was a lovely idea when I mentioned we might get our own bedroom to share, just the two of us. What I didn't say was that I was also hoping that we could share a bed.

My stomach flipped with the possibility. Linking arms with Linda was the best feeling in the world and the next step was to feel her whole body against mine.

Before the holiday, Mum told me that we were moving out of the flat. As I packed my new swimming costume, a towel, a change of clothes, two pairs of socks, two pairs of knickers, my washbag and dictionary, Mum explained that I was to telephone my sister when I got back and that she would pass on details of our new place.

'There's nowhere lined up at the minute, but there will be. You go and enjoy yourself.'

Mum didn't realise that I had other things on my mind than where I was going to be living. I couldn't stop thinking about Linda and what it would be like to kiss her.

The journey to Devon was endless. My fantasy of a minibus with pairs of padded seats was replaced with the reality of a windowless converted van with hard, wooden benches screwed to either side. Ten girls were squeezed into the airless back, cut off from the youth club leader and her boyfriend, who was driving, by a partition of grubby white-painted steel. I had imagined I would be sitting next to Linda and pretending we were a band on tour, but because she was so popular I didn't even get to squash beside her.

A girl was sick into a carrier bag and the sweet cloying smell fixed itself into the lining of my nose. I didn't care about any of the others. I disliked one girl in particular who became judge and jury on what we looked like when we dozed off. She declared me the worst-looking sleeper because my mouth hung open as I slept. I was horrified that Linda had seen me like that and made sure I didn't fall asleep again on the journey.

We arrived at the holiday apartment, where I claimed the small room with bunk beds for Linda and me. It wasn't a double bed, but at least it was our own room.

'Top or bottom?' Linda asked.

'You choose,' I said.

She took the top.

*

I sat down on the beach, took my jelly sandals and socks off, rested my feet in the warm, gritty sand, tilted my face to the sapphire sky and closed my eyes. Sunlight made the back of my eyelids pink and I could see threads of veins. My pulse throbbed in my ears and the sea sounded like passing traffic. I opened my eyes to the brightness. A breeze lifted Linda's hair around her face. She looked like a lion and everything around me smelt so clean. I grabbed her hand and pulled her with me towards the ocean. We stopped at the edge, where it lapped at our bare feet, and looked at each other.

'We only live once!' I said, stepping into the water.

'I can't swim, you know,' she said.

'Don't worry, neither can I.'

We held hands and waded in to our waists, letting the waves splash us. Linda laughed, and I could see she had lots of grey metal fillings, which glinted preciously in the sunlight. I licked the briny taste of the sea from my lips. Linda slicked her wet hair back, tight and gleaming on her skull. Fine blond hairs stood up and shone on the nape of her neck. She squinted and held her hand to her forehead to shade the sun from her eyes, which were greener than I had ever seen them.

A fierce wave sent us reeling in squealing terror back to shore. We flung ourselves down on the sand and giggled. The other girls circled us.

'What yer like!'

Linda's wet blouse was translucent and her sharp, pink nipples pushed against the material. I tore my gaze away, to her feet, to her long straight toes, wiggling freely in her flip-flops.

Linda helped me to hunt for my missing white ankle sock with the red pompom on the back, part of a brand-new pair bought for the holiday. She treated the search as though it was a treasure hunt. As we passed sandcastles and moats I thought about the car Dad

157

had once built out of wet sand on Margate beach. Big enough to sit in, it had front seats, back seats, a bonnet, a boot, wheels, a bucket steering wheel and a spade gear stick. Somewhere, though maybe it had been lost or burnt, there was a photograph of me in the driver's seat. My hands were on the wheel, a proud grin on my face. It was not everybody's dad that could build a car out of sand, that's what I was thinking as I had posed for the camera, and what I was thinking now. Two unknown boys sat in the back, and beside the car stood a woman, their mother probably, her head crowned by a precarious beehive hairdo.

'I give up!' Linda said, cheerfully. 'It's gone to sock heaven!'

We joined the other girls and went to the pictures to see the Sex Pistols in *The Great Rock 'n' Roll Swindle*. In the interest of fairness, which is how she put it, Linda sat between two other girls. When Johnny Rotten looked from the screen and said that when you reach twenty-nine and you've got two kids all you would end up wanting to do is commit suicide, I wished that Linda was beside me so I could squeeze her hand.

Even though I was desperate to be alone with Linda, we spent our days and nights with the other girls. As a gang, we met skinheads, punks and lads that, according to their mates, didn't know how to read and were *mazed*, which seemed to mean mad, although when I looked it up in my dictionary it wasn't there. Everyone had funny accents and called us 'maids'. People didn't say, 'Where's that?' when we told them where we were from, they said, 'Where's that to?' and that didn't make sense to us. Stockport wasn't *to* anywhere, it just was. We decided Devon was truly bizarre and wrote a postcard to John Peel at Radio 1 telling him so, in the hope he'd read it out live on air.

At night I thought of Linda sleeping gently above me on the top bunk. I wondered what she would do if I joined her. I was not exactly sure what I would do if I got there, but I knew that I wanted to breathe in her warm, sunny, sandy smell and hold her close. Every night I thought about climbing the wooden rungs and slipping under the covers next to her, but I never did. I always buried my face in the pillow as I tried to sleep, hoping that Linda would never catch me with my mouth hanging open.

On the last night I asked her if we could spend the evening together without the others. She started to say it wasn't fair to the rest of the girls, but I quickly told her I was depressed and that I needed to be on my own with her and she became gravely serious and nodded.

'Of course,' she said. 'Tonight's just for you.'

We walked arm in arm towards the beach and I looked down at my pale arm pressed along the golden sheen of hers.

I wondered if it was the right moment to suggest we share a bed. I was about to ask when two lads, their hair cut millimetres from their scalps, their nails clean and square cut, appeared out of nowhere and ruined the moment. It turned out they were on leave from the army. Even though they weren't in uniform, they swaggered as though they were and I wanted to shoot them.

Linda sat on the beach with one soldier and I sat with the other. I barely talked but Linda chatted. It killed me to see her like that.

'Linda,' I said.

She didn't hear me.

'Linda,' I said, louder.

She broke off her conversation and gave me a puzzled look.

'Shall we get going?' I said.

'What?'

'We have to meet the others, *remember*?'

'No we don't.'

Why was Linda always so honest? It must have been her Christian outlook. I was about to say that I really needed to have a word with her when her soldier began to kiss her. She let him. I had never seen Linda necking before and it surprised me that she looked so used to it. She wrapped her arms around him and pulled him closer.

'Linda!' I shouted.

She stopped and turned around.

'I really need to talk.'

She bit her lip and for a moment I thought that I had won her back. But then she shrugged.

'We'll have a really good chat tomorrow, Ann, honest.'

'But you promised!'

Linda waved her hand, an apologetic dismissal. She got up and walked away arm in arm with her soldier. I lost her in the dunes.

Annoyed that Linda had gone off with her soldier, I decided to kiss my soldier. His lips wrapped around mine and his fumbling, eager hands darting about my body bored me. I closed my eyes and pictured a photograph of Dad I'd seen once; he was wearing a uniform with shiny buttons and a diagonally-worn soft looking hat. When I'd asked him about it he told me that most men his age had done National Service, which was like being in the army. Dad had worn another uniform too, though I'd never seen it. My sister had told me that he had been a prison officer. But when I asked Dad about it his face clouded over and I knew not to ask again. Did working behind bars do your head in that badly? Was that part of what made him do what he did?

'I can't believe you're only fourteen,' the soldier said, pausing for breath.

He pulled me to the ground and lowered his body on top of mine and his weight pressed me into the sand as he wormed his urgent tongue into my mouth. How far was Linda going to go with her soldier? I watched the yellow full moon bright in the sky, hidden now and again behind drifting luminous clouds. It felt like the soldier was starting to suck blood from my neck, but I didn't care, I would comb the bites out in the van on the way home like Helen had taught me to do years ago. He lifted my skirt and worked his fingers into my knickers and inside me, pushing them deeper and deeper. I moaned because I knew he would like that.

'Let's do it,' he said and then added, as an afterthought, 'Please.'

I wondered if I should.

'Go on,' he said.

He started to beg, which really put me off and then he kneeled beside me and his underpants were down. And there it was, in a nest of dark blond hair. Glistening. I'd never looked at one so closely before. It looked back at me with its slit, lidless eye and waved a little. His balls were not at all what I thought they would look like. I had imagined two separate and distinct round spheres either side but they weren't exactly round and they were in a tight bag of skin covered in hair.

The soldier pushed my head down. I closed my eyes and pretended my mouth was a hand and tasted salt. What would I do when all that white stuff exploded in me? I tried not to think about it. I thought about the kinds of things the other soldier was doing to Linda. It didn't seem right. I pulled away before that stuff choked me to death.

'What is it?' he said.

'I better get off.'

I stood up and the soldier zipped up and stood up next to me, slinging his arm around my shoulders.

'I hope Linda's all right,' I said.

On cue I heard Linda's voice. She stepped out of darkness onto the moonlit beach with her soldier.

'What's the time?' I asked.

'Bang on midnight,' my soldier said.

'We're supposed to be back now,' I said.

Linda looked dreamily into her soldier's eyes.

'I better be going, Nigel,' she said.

I didn't even know the name of my lad. Had he told me? I didn't remember and I didn't care. The soldiers walked us back to the apartment and we necked our goodbyes before they reluctantly left and we waved them off like they were going to war.

Later, when Linda was in her bunk I asked her what she had done with Nigel; a crap name if ever I'd heard one.

'Just hung out in the dunes, nothing much,' she said.

Was she telling the truth? I wasn't sure. But I felt strangely left out. If she had gone all the way with her soldier then I should have gone and done it with mine.

*

In the morning, the youth club leader looked startled by the love-bites on my neck, but she didn't say anything. They didn't matter, anyway. I knew that they would be gone before I got back to Stockport, all I had to do was comb them so they'd resemble a natural rash. We all went for one last walk to the beach. There we found, mashed into wet sand, but sticking out because of the red pompom, my missing sock. None of us could believe that it hadn't been swept away. I took it as a sign from God that I would get together with Linda. I just had to be patient.

On the journey home I combed my lovebites and mulled over whether Linda had actually got swept away and done it with her lad. She fell asleep and was voted the most angelic looking sleeper. The more I thought about it, the more I decided that it was ridiculous to even think that she had done much with Nigel. When the van dropped me in Mersey Square, Linda was groggy with sleep, and looked so innocent when she said goodbye that I realised she was definitely not the type to go all the way with a lad.

As I crossed the road to the phone box my suitcase broke. I looked down at the sky blue curve of handle left in my hand. The rest of the case flopped slowly onto its leatherette side. I looked around at the orange-lit square and beyond, to the red-brick viaduct, the biggest in the world, I'd heard, made up of millions of bricks, and all at once the weight of not knowing where I lived fell on me. I wanted a house, a home, a front gate, a cat, a bed, a dad – and not just any dad, my dad.

I kicked the edge of my suitcase towards the telephone box. I opened the red door and stepped inside. I unfolded a scrap of paper with my sister's number on it. I phoned the operator and reversed the charges. Susan answered and said that Mum had decided that we were going to be staying at hers for a bit and that I should get a taxi to her flat. Susan said that she would wait outside with the money to pay for it.

*

Mum was sitting on the settee in Susan's lounge. I could tell things weren't going well by her faraway gaze. I discovered a cardboard box she had packed with things I might need and I pulled out my school uniform. I put a towel on the floor, laid out my uniform on top and sponged it clean with a damp dishcloth and ironed it dry and flat. School was on the horizon. At least it was something to do.

For a few days I slept on cushions on the floor next to the settee where Mum slept, but the sounds of her sleeping kept waking me up and I didn't want to share a room with her anyway, so I dragged the cushions into the kitchen and wedged them into the small space. I found it easy to sleep there, lulled by the gentle hum of the fridge.

*

Back at school I was allocated CSE classes and only put into GSE classes for English and Art. I took this as evidence that the school had no idea who I was. I knew I wasn't thick and that Dad would have been disappointed that I was in the bottom classes, but I was never going to show anybody that I cared, though the news had brought on a headache unlike any I'd ever had before.

The distance from school to Susan's flat was miles and I could hardly build up the energy to catch the two buses to get me back. The second bus I caught terminated early and I walked the rest of the way in the rain. My head felt elastic and stretched with thoughts that kept snapping. My bag of schoolbooks felt heavier with each step.

As I trudged alongside cars that were speeding towards warm houses, cooked dinners, happy families and soft, furry pets, I knew I was literally on the road to nowhere. Maybe I really was stupid. Sleeping on the kitchen floor was my future and I was living in a fantasy if I thought I ever had a chance of being a pop star.

I stopped by a deep murky puddle in the road and waited. Cars avoided it but when a lorry came along and drove through it, the water rose in a slick oily curtain and smacked me. I dripped and squelched my way to Susan's flat, half wishing that I'd had the nerve to step off the pavement and stand in front of the lorry and end it all. The front door key was under a stone in front of the house as Mum thought it was common to have a key on a string around my neck.

When I got in, she was dozing, curled on her side on the settee. She hadn't been going into work lately. I stood in front of her and thought how I must look like a drowned rat. Then I began to wonder where that expression had come from. Who had used it first and how come everybody started to use it? And why did I care anyway? My own voice inside my head was getting on my nerves. It dawned on me that I no longer had conversations with God and God no longer had conversations with me.

I shook Mum awake. 'I've got a really bad headache, Mum,' I said.

She looked drowsily at me and sat up.

'I promise you,' she said, 'I'll get things sorted.'

*

When I got back from school the next day, Mum was standing waiting by the door.

'I got us somewhere! I spent the morning looking. We're off. Right now. Get your things, Ann. This is it! I've done it.'

It was a boarding house on the A6, and Mum and I were sharing an attic bedroom.

That night, I lay there in the single bed opposite her bed, looking at the bland slope of ceiling above me, listening to the traffic hurtling past, thinking of all those people going places.

brynn

She looks in a newsagent's window at the white cards with handwritten adverts for used bicycles and odd-job men and rooms to let. For some reason she begins to cry and can't seem to stop. The shopkeeper comes outside and brings her inside and sits her on a chair and makes her a sugary cup of tea.

The shopkeeper gets out of her that she is searching for a place to live with her daughter. From the window he takes a card advertising rooms in a boarding house and shows it her. She tells him it isn't suitable, she's looking to rent a two-bedroom flat. He says it will probably be fine for getting on with, and, after some persuasion on his part, she eventually agrees that after all it is only for the interim.

She sits there drinking the sweet tea while the shopkeeper serves a customer cigarettes. A memory comes to her from the time before the psoriasis appeared. She'd been pregnant with Rob and she'd gone to a sauna for the first time and fainted. The woman there had given her a soft-boiled egg to revive her. It was the best egg she'd ever eaten. She hadn't known she was pregnant but the woman hinted as much. It's funny how she still thinks of her – bending over with the egg, long, deep lines from the corner of her nose to her mouth, filled with brown nicotine.

The newsagent comes back from serving his customer and suggests she use his telephone to call the boarding house. She doesn't like being pressured, but he dials the number and she speaks to the landlady – a nicely-spoken woman called Shirley. She books a room with two single beds, full board. As she leaves the shop she reminds herself never to come this way again.

a little life

The steam rose from the electric kettle. 'When I was pregnant with Rob,' Mum said, 'I had a sauna and fainted. The manageress of the place gave me a soft-boiled egg to revive me.' Mum had a kind of longing in her voice that I didn't understand. It was only an egg, after all.

The kettle switch clicked off. Mum put it on to boil again. We were in the room reserved for guests, cooking eggs inside the kettle for our tea. Shirley, who had turned into the meanest landlady in the world, according to Mum, barged in with two plates and set them down on the table in front of us.

'Just making a cup of tea,' Mum said, looking guilty.

'Spaghetti bolognese. My best dish,' Shirley said, and then winked at me. I looked down at my plate. I was used to spaghetti out of a tin – short, red and normal-looking; this looked long, ill and anaemic. Shirley left the room and came back with a small pot that looked like a saltshaker.

'Go easy with this, it costs a fortune.'

As Shirley left, I examined the label.

'What is it? Something foreign?' Mum asked.

'Parmesan cheese.'

For a few minutes, we twirled our forks in the food. Mum tried a mouthful and chewed it with a sour face.

'Muck,' she said. 'Have you noticed that Shirley doesn't feed her family what she gives us? They're always wolfing down Kentucky Fried Chicken. It's very expensive that, you know.'

Mum passed me a hard-boiled egg and I peeled it and dropped the shell onto my plate. I bit into the glossy whiteness of the egg and looked at the yellow, liquid centre. There was a banging sound from the kitchen.

'Better hurry!' Mum said.

We popped the rest of the eggs into our mouths at the same time. Still swallowing, I unfolded the local newspaper and we scraped Shirley's food from our plates onto the centre pages. I folded the food away and hid the newspaper package behind the settee, ready to take later to a bin a few streets away.

'You enjoyed that then,' Shirley said, when she came to collect our empty plates.

'Delicious,' Mum said.

'I know.' Shirley laughed. 'Shouldn't go saying it myself.'

We were the only guests in the house. I asked Shirley if I could have my own bedroom since there were so many empty ones, but Shirley said no. She said a guest could ring up at any time, and every room had to be ready for last-minute bookings.

Although our room did have a sink, it was rare that the water was hot in the morning. Shirley would grudgingly put the immersion heater on for twenty minutes when we requested our weekly bath allowance, but that was all. 'She's a miserly so and so,' Mum moaned, though she never complained to Shirley.

The baffling thing was that Mum seemed happier. She was getting sociable with Shirley, even though she said she didn't really like her. Then Mum managed to get her old job back working at the market research company. On weekends I worked there too.

*

'So she said a couple of lesbians had moved in next door, turned out she meant Lebanese!'

The office erupted into laughter and I looked around at all the women. There were no men, because Dolores the supervisor had got around equal opportunities at the Job Centre by pretending that the office only had a female toilet.

Because I was fourteen and not a trained interviewer, my role was to call people up and recite the opening part of the interview script. I used my posh phone voice and thought of the way Dad had liked me to say things.

'Hello my name is Ann Westbourne and I am calling from Moor Marketing Research.'

Sometimes the phone would be put down before I'd finished saying 'hello'. Other times, I lasted a little longer, but it was hard to find a person who was willing to talk and who had also seen the advert in question on the television. The few times that happened I was triumphant, like I had scored a winning goal. My job was done.

'Please wait a moment while I pass you to an experienced interviewer.'

I would jam my hand over the receiver and wave in all directions. A free interviewer would hurry over to finish the survey while I took her place.

Dolores often took a break from supervising the office so that she could phone home to talk to her two wolfhounds. According to Audrey, who took pride in being regarded as the best interviewer by Dolores – and had even been invited to her house – Dolores doted on her dogs in the way she did because she was unable to have children. This all stemmed from her husband's first wife stabbing her in the stomach out of jealousy.

'Her dogs go and see a psychiatrist,' Audrey told me.

'You're joking?'

'No, not at all. It's the truth, pure and simple,' she said.

I looked at Dolores and wondered what she could have done to her dogs that they needed to go to a psychiatrist.

And then I looked at Mum and wondered what she had done to Dad.

Mum was on the phone in the middle of saying 'advertisements'. She was always criticising the way some of the others in the office pronounced it, but she only disapproved of their pronunciation behind their backs, never to their faces. Why could she never say it to them? She would be charming at work and then as soon as we left her face would fall and she would gripe about all of them. It was exhausting. Why did everyone fall short of Mum's expectations? Why couldn't she make friends with them?

'Would you say you thought it was excellent, very good, good, neither good nor bad…'

Had it got Dad down too, that Mum was so picky over people? Was it all her fault?

'Anything else you recall?'

Mum tugged the hem of her dress over her American Tan covered knees. She was getting bigger and her body stretched the seams of her dress, which had once been baggy. I hoped I would never get fat like her.

'And what is the occupation of the head of the household?'

She put down the phone and checked her paperwork. She glanced out of the window at the line of trees losing their leaves and becoming lean. Her smile slipped and she circled the gold band of her wedding ring with her thumb and index finger. What on earth was Mum thinking about? Was she thinking about Dad? About what she had done to him?

The psoriasis on her wrists stared at me and I switched from blaming Mum to feeling sorry for her. I was horrible. She was trying her best. Not only did she have this job, she was cleaning all the offices in the building as well. She was doing so much to make ends meet. She probably saw me as an ungrateful so-and-so. I remembered being little and Mum showing me how to catch the fluffy seeds from a dandelion clock that blew in the wind. She told me the seeds were fairies and gave me a matchbox with sugar in it for the fairies to live in, and she used to put lemon in my hair to make it go blond.

There was another time, sharp in my mind; Mum picking me up from infants' school early, telling the teacher that I had a dentist's appointment, but when we got outside she burst into tears and it turned out I didn't really have to see the dentist. When I got home I realised that Dad wasn't there. He'd gone off again.

What sort of a life has Mum had since Dad has gone? What sort of life did she have with him when he was alive? What sort of life was she having with me? I felt bad.

'You okay, Mum?' I asked.

She turned to me and faintly smiled across the clutter of voices.

'Better be getting on!' she said.

brynn

She thinks of herself as heartbroken, but that sounds like something from one of those romantic paperbacks and it's nothing like that.

She remembers after she'd learnt to drive she got a job that came with a minivan, delivering catalogue goods. One time she wondered if he really was playing table tennis quite so much after work, and so she followed him. She saw him open the door for the other woman to get into his car and she drove behind them until they stopped at a hotel. They'd only ever stayed in a hotel for one night on their honeymoon and here he was willy-nilly going to one with a common-looking woman. And where the hell did the money come from? It had to come from somewhere and if that woman was paying for it that was disgusting.

When she saw them come out of the hotel she wanted to press her horn hard and for a long time, but she didn't. She did think of ramming the minivan into them both and then she thought of driving off and never stopping and leaving everyone behind. She decided then and there that she would leave him, that she was going to end the marriage and walk off, and he'd be landed with the kids to slave over. She was twenty-eight years old and she was going to show him that she wasn't going to be taken for a ride any more. She'd had it.

The woman he'd chosen wasn't even beautiful or pretty or attractive. Her neck was stringy and she was too tall for a woman. Her clothes were ill-fitting and the wrong colour. Back then she thought he had broken her heart. She never realised that her heart was only fractured and that one day it would be properly broken – so much so that it could never be mended and it would be impossible to ever take him back again.

always another one

I had never expected to see Mickey again, but one day she suddenly appeared – back from Morecambe – and the warts from her fingers had vanished. I made no mention of the scabies that she had given me before she left, as I didn't want anything to get in the way of the chances of her sliding her hand between my legs again.

'There were nowt to do. I just kept on sleepin',' she said when I asked about Morecambe.

This surprised me, as everyone knew Morecambe had slot machines and funfairs. Mickey's mum was still there, living with her good-looking TV salesman boyfriend, but was due to come back soon. Meanwhile Mickey was living with her nan.

'Does that mean you'll be charging off to Brinnington at all hours?' Mum said, when I told her Mickey had come back. Brinnington was under a mile away but Mum saw it as another world that wasn't as good as ours because it was full of council houses. We lived in a boarding house and I had free school meals, so as far as I could see we weren't any different to the people in Brinnington. I reckoned my mother looked down on them because people in Brinny seemed to say what they really thought, unlike Mum.

*

Mickey unfolded a camp bed and put it next to hers when I stayed over. The image of sharing her bed crumbled and I felt desperate but bold. I needed to feel her hand reach out for me. She flung an old blanket over her bed and a new looking blanket over my bed.

'Remember that other time?' I asked.

'What time?' she said, vaguely.

Did she really not remember? Or was she embarrassed? Maybe she wanted to forget about it. Or perhaps she secretly hoped it would happen again? She turned the light off, and the spill of streetlight cast an orange glow over the room. I stood awkwardly and watched her strip to her underwear, and thought of her soft skin rubbing against mine, her wandering hand waking me in the night.

I gulped air. 'Could I get in with yer?' I said.

Mickey was quiet and frozen. She got under her covers and rolled to the edge of the wall, out of reach, and only the cold silence pressed against me. I stayed in my clothes, got under the blanket on my camp bed and felt the chill.

*

At five in the morning Mickey's alarm clock shrilled into the darkness. She was back doing an early shift at her old job at the cafe. She scrambled out from the end of her bed and pulled her clothes on and left. I climbed into her warm bed, thinking about her, wishing that I could melt into her skin without her realising.

When I was leaving, Mickey's nan pressed some coins into my hand. 'There yer go, some spends,' she said. I refused as it didn't seem right, what with Mickey slaving away at work and Mum thinking that we were better than Brinnington people.

'Don't go looking a gift horse in the mouth,' said her nan, as though she knew what I was thinking.

So I took it. I didn't want to seem rude. On the bus on the way home I rubbed the cool coins between my palms and thought how kind Mickey's nan was and how my mum had it all wrong about people from Brinny.

Mickey didn't invite me over again. She never did talk to me about what I had asked her, and no rumours began at school, so she didn't go telling anyone else either. It was a secret, but not an exciting one, between us – it was just something that had never happened. I decided I had to look elsewhere for a girl that wouldn't refuse.

*

I went to gigs as much as I could, catching the 192 bus into Manchester to a basement club called Rafters, where the doorman would let me in for free. This is where I met Laura. She was twenty-one and drove a red Mini. She gave me a lift home in it the first time I met her. I put my hand on her knee and she didn't push it away.

'I'm a feminist,' she told me.

'What's that?'

'I believe in women's liberation.'

'Oh, like women's lib?'

I checked to see if she was wearing a bra. She wasn't.

I told her about all the things I believed in.

'That's socialism,' she said.

We both leant over the handbrake and necked for ages, and then I went home and looked up *socialism* in the dictionary.

It was Laura who introduced me properly to the clitoris. She worked for a feminist fanzine and nestled within the pages was a photograph of a vagina that named all the parts. I was alarmed but intrigued to discover that the vagina was only one of the names for what lay beneath my triangle of hair: Clitoris, Mons Pubis, Labium Majora, Labium Minora, Urethra. There were so many things that I hadn't really thought about. Had the tampon illustration I'd followed shown all these things? It hadn't shown the clitoris, I was sure of that.

'The clit's only use is for pleasure.' Laura smiled. 'Isn't that amazing?'

Laura visited the Lesbian and Gay Advice Centre to find out about the age of consent for lesbians, seeing as I was only fourteen. They told her there were no rules for females, as, when the laws of homosexuality were being made, Queen Victoria couldn't understand what two women would do together. The worker at the centre told Laura that seeing as she was twenty-one and I was fourteen there might be issues of corruption of a minor, but Laura said that was unlikely as I was as up for it as she was. We decided we were officially going out together.

*

When I ran into Mickey in Mersey Square, I resisted the urge to tell her that I was going out with a girl who was twenty-one.

'I'm on the way to visit me nan in hospital,' Mickey said.

'What's a matter?'

'Women's business. Down there.'

I tried not to think of what that could mean, or which part it actually applied to.

'Will yer come with us, Ann?'

'There's nothing to properly worry about is there?' I asked, hoping that this was the case.

'They say they do the op all the time,' Mickey said in a thin, shaky voice.

'There you go. Sounds routine to me. I'm on me way somewhere.' I was going to Laura's house. We were going to have sex for the first time.

'Please, Ann, I'm just feeling dead panicked about it,' Mickey said.

'I can't. Soz. I'll come next week.'

Mickey turned around and headed to the bus station. I watched her shrink into the distance and wondered whether I should go with her after all.

'It'll be all right,' I shouted instead, though I wasn't sure if she heard me or not.

*

Laura lived in a shared house and when I arrived she guided me into the lounge to meet her housemates. Thet were sitting on the wooden floorboards, gathered around a saucepan of stew, made with what they told me was textured vegetable protein. They assumed I was there to join in the meal, so I sat on the floor, dreading that if it tasted anything like it looked, I was going to be poisoned. I was used to eating toast, boiled eggs, fish and chips, salt and vinegar crisps and school dinners, and the look of this food made me nauseous. I pushed it around my plate, trying to understand the animated conversation going on around me, which a man introduced to me as John was at the centre of.

John was peering intensely at Laura through his round, thick, wire-rimmed glasses.

'Employment is just exploitation,' he said.

'You're always going on about class oppression but you never mention the women,' Laura said. 'Let's face it, they're far more oppressed than any man. Not just at work but –'

'Come on Laura, the origins of women's oppression are class-ridden,' John said.

'I think it would suit all men if women had their babies and cooked their dinners.'

'When did I ever say anything like that?' John said.

'I didn't mean you.'

'You're always twisting what I say.'

John lapsed into showy silence, while Laura began to stack the plates noisily. I stood up with mine, but Laura gestured for me to sit down again.

'Relax,' she said, then looked at my full plate. 'Didn't you like it?'

'I just weren't that hungry,' I lied, adding, with what I hoped was a seductive smile, 'I've got other things on my mind.'

Laura didn't seem to notice my smile or my words. She looked over at John instead.

'You know that the word family comes from the Latin and it means slaves,' Laura said to him. 'It means slaves that belong to one man.'

'And what's that supposed to mean?' he said.

Together, they stepped into the hallway with the plates. I listened to the sound of their argument trailing away as they got to the kitchen. The remaining housemates picked up the discussion about oppression, repression, the workers and the ruling class. I shut out their words, which meant nothing to me, and instead began to daydream about having sex with Laura. The endless conversation kept interfering with my thoughts, and even though I felt awkward leaving the room with everyone watching me, I went to look for the real thing instead.

But she wasn't in the kitchen. I went out into the hallway and climbed the stairs. When I got to the top, there was a room opposite, the door was ajar and I heard Laura. I pushed the door open wider and there she was, her naked back to me, astride John, also naked. Under the stark overhead bulb she was swaying back and forth, riding him like a horse. She was going quite fast and his glasses were flung to the floor. He stared blindly in my direction. I watched briefly, feeling the injustice of the situation and feeling overwhelming misery, before going back to the lounge.

I sat back down with the others, who all at once seemed so much older than I was. No one talked to me and I felt like I didn't belong. I picked at a splinter of floorboard and thought that if Dad hadn't done what he did, I would not be here, I wouldn't be in this situation. It was his fault. Then I felt guilty I'd even thought like that. This situation was entirely my fault and it was cowardly of me to blame him. I looked around at the housemates, wondering if I could blame one of them instead.

'Is she up there with John?' a housemate asked.

I nodded.

'They used to go out,' she said.

That was news to me. I thought Laura was a lesbian and not only that, I thought she was my girlfriend. The housemate came and sat next to me and in the midst of my confusion it occurred to me that her bust was very small considering how fat she was. Not wanting her to think I was in the least bothered that she was fat or Laura was with John, I stroked her pink blotchy arm. She looked down at my hand and then at me.

'Should we go to bed?' I asked.

She grinned, took my hand and led me up to her room.

She was twenty-four and a teacher, and, as she turned on her bedside lamp and took her clothes off, she seemed untroubled by her dimpled body and the white stretch marks that tracked her flesh like opened-up dress seams. She helped me take my clothes off, and I felt shy.

Early the next morning I crept from the room and down the stairs. The house was drowsy and still and I didn't want to interrupt it. I pulled the door lightly shut behind me and stepped into an outside world that didn't seem quite right. It was as though I was on a film set and if I pushed against any one of the houses or trees that I walked by, I would find they were made out of wood and paint.

Later that day Laura phoned me. I stood in the hall, twisting the curly payphone cord around my finger.

'I'm sorry about John,' she said. 'I never meant for you to think you and I were monogamous. The thing is, I don't know how to tell you this…'

'Go on,' I said, knowing something bad was coming.

'I've got back together with him.'

'Ta, then,' I said, putting the receiver down on her.

I looked up *monogamous* in the dictionary and wrote down the definition in my notebook. One day I intended to make use of the words I was collecting. The only thing that I had managed to write so far though didn't amount to much and was about school. *Brash youths hard faced and hard fisted drag their dreary feet on the hard floors.* I needed to expand my vocabulary. I glanced through some of the words that I had recently collected: *Slattern: Untidy or slovenly woman. Heinous: Atrocious. Chimera: Wild Scheme. Pluvial: Caused by rain. Snicker: Laugh slyly. Vortex: Whirling motion. Perturb: Throw into disquiet.*

*

The weekend was over and had not been what I'd expected. I met Mickey crossing the school playing field.

'How's yer nan?' I asked.

'Dead,' Mickey said in a flat voice as though she wasn't bothered. She began to chew the edges of her thumbnail.

'But I thought…'

'There were complications at hospital. I knew in me bones summat would happen. They're investigating.'

It was so hard to find the right words to say. Saying sorry just didn't seem enough. A vision of Mickey's nan came into my mind, a plain, solid woman. Mickey had once told me that her nan's favourite thing was to stretch out on top of her bed naked to dry off after a bath, and we had laughed at the disturbing image of her nan without clothes on. Now it seemed cruel to have laughed. Why hadn't I gone to the hospital with Mickey? I thought of her nan pressing the coins into my hands.

'She were dead kind,' I said.

'Yeah,' Mickey said, 'I wish I hadn't been so tight with her now. Before she went in the hospital we had an argument about summat or other, I can't even remember what it were now, and I nicked her glasses and she were chasing me down street to get 'em back. I remember looking behind and she was right out of breath.'

Mickey scraped the raw pad of her nail through her front teeth.

'Is your mam back from Morecambe?' I asked.

'She doesn't want to leave her boyfriend – he's moved into video players and cameras now, but I'm not going back there. I've gone into care,' she said. 'It's not that bad to tell yer truth. Me mam bought me loads of clothes and whatnot. I've got more things than ever. It's a right laugh really.'

But I could see her eyes were watery. 'Bloody wind always blowin' grit,' she said.

a new start

'I'm going to buy this place off Shirley,' Mum announced as I came through the front door and dropped my school bag to the floor. 'I'm going to call it Dandelion Guest House. She's leaving the furniture and I'll get continental quilts from the Co-op for all the beds.'

'But where'll the money come from?' I asked.

'Rob's guaranteeing a bank loan.'

My head spun with the thought of the boarding house being ours thanks to my brother. I couldn't quite picture it. Mum combed her fingers through her perm.

'Six pounds a night for bed, breakfast and evening meal! We'll be rolling in it before you know it! And you'll have your own room.'

Mum made a shopping trip to the Co-op and bought everything we needed on hire purchase. She tracked down and bought a visitors' book for the guests to sign and took out an advert in the local paper, which, with a dash of pride, she cut out to keep.

For the first time in months I had my own room and I lay on my bed and listened to the sound of my own breathing. Mum, not wanting to take up a bedroom that could be let, slept on the settee in the lounge. We waited for the payphone in the hall to ring and for our first booking.

Soon our house was full of men.

*

'Do you know what this road is known as?' Frank asked. We were standing at the doorstep on a cold autumnal evening, watching a police car speed by.

'The A6?' I said.

'It's known as the spine of England,' he told me. 'It's the longest road we've got.'

It was the same main road that Dad had driven me down the last day I was with him. I squinted my eyes to try and see a flash of Dad driving by with me in the passenger seat, sucking the ends of my hair into points.

'You okay?' Frank asked.

I widened my eyes. I didn't want to appear abnormal in front of him. Not Frank. He was not like the other men that stayed. They were all labourers in dirty overalls, whereas Frank wore a suit and tie. He had soft hands and long fingers with clean, oval nails. He was an engineer, preparing plans for a future road.

'He gets a proper hotel allowance, you know,' Mum said. 'But Frank prefers to lodge with us because it's more homely.'

Frank stayed weekdays and headed home at weekends, back to his wife and children. I wondered enviously what they all did together when he got home, but I never asked. In my head, Frank was sort of my dad on weekdays, and that meant we should do things together. Dad had taught me to play cards and so I bought a new pack so I could play with Frank. Every time I saw him I wanted to ask if we could play gin rummy, but never did. What if he said no? I couldn't stand the thought.

I took the four kings from the pack and staggered them vertically in my hand, so that the top of each king popped out from behind another. I told my imaginary audience that the kings had arrived at a hotel and were going to stay in various rooms. I placed the kings face down on top of the remaining stack of cards, which I explained was the hotel. I slotted three of the kings into random floors of the pack. At this point my audience was only seeing the back of the card, but they would know that they were the kings I had previously shown them. I kept the final king on top of the stack. I informed my audience that after a good night's sleep, the king of hearts on the top floor wanted everyone to join him at the top. I lifted him up and knocked three times on the pack. Turning the top cards one by one, all the kings had miraculously risen to the top of the deck again.

Dad had taught me this.

The trick was to hide three face cards behind the staggered kings when you showed the cards to the audience, so that the cards you slid into the deck were not the kings at all. They only seemed like they were.

*

Our next door neighbour, Rita, began to pop round on a daily basis. Rita was fat with lank greasy black hair, wore bright caftans and was always on the lookout for bacon. Her husband Duncan wouldn't let her buy any, as he said it was too expensive.

Rita would sit on the floor with her legs open wide, her caftan tucked up high between her bare thighs, a plate of Mum's crispy bacon between them, and talk nonstop as though she wasn't used to it. She would sometimes confide in us about her love life with Duncan. We didn't really want to hear, but we listened anyway.

'I never wear knickers yer know,' she told us. 'Duncan won't allow it.' Her husband Duncan was slight and grey with a high, thin voice. I couldn't imagine him laying down the law.

'I'd love to lose a bit of weight but me boobs might get smaller and Duncan wouldn't approve.'

*

I babysat for Rita and Duncan one night. Their daughter was named June, after the month she was conceived, nine years before and was already in bed when I got there, so I had a snoop around the house.

Duncan had turned one of the bedrooms into a library. Rita had warned me that he didn't like anyone to touch the books but I pushed the door open, stepped inside and ran my fingers firmly across the leatherette spines and golden titles of the volumes. I took out Charles Dickens' *Great Expectations* and sat down on the large wicker chair placed in the centre of the room, feeling like I was about to appear on *Jackanory*.

I opened the stiff cover and began to read: *My father's family name being Pirrip, and my Christian name Philip, my infant tongue could make of both names nothing longer or more explicit than Pip.* I didn't get any further. I heard banging from upstairs. Carefully, I put the book back, positioning it so it became exactly level with the other books.

I headed up the staircase to June's bedroom. This part of the stairs was carpeted with brown cord, as, according to Duncan, there was no point continuing the plush maroon carpet up to a kid's room, as visitors would never see it.

June was sitting up in bed. Her soggy eyes followed me as I entered the room and she kept banging her head hard against the wall. I asked her what she was doing but she carried on banging and didn't reply for a while. Maybe she was weighing up if she could trust me or not.

'It's the only way I can stop it.'

'What?'

She tapped her head with her fingers.

'It's like bricks hitting bruises inside me head.'

She began to cry. I sat on the edge of her bed. She rested her head on the pillow and I stroked her greasy hair, the only feature where she took after her mother.

'Mum's always on settee eating sweets when I get in from school. She makes me go down cellar and get pies out of freezer and put them in oven for our tea.'

'What else does she make yer do?'

'Everything. She don't do nowt. And he's not me real dad yer know so that's why he goes around hating me.'

'Where's your real dad?'

'I'm not sure, but I know he'll come and get me one day.'

June closed her eyes and I carried on stroking her thin strands of hair. I watched her eyelids quiver as she fell into sleep. I decided that maybe there was something worse than having a dead dad and that would be to have Duncan as a stepdad.

*

Mum was flushed and girlish. She gestured at the back room with her hand. She tried to speak but spluttered with laughter and buried her face in the back of the settee to drown it out. She lifted her head up.

'Mum, you're drunk!'

She struggled to compose herself before she began to speak again.

'She's, you know…'

'Who? What?'

'You know!'

'No, I don't know.'

'Rita… with Frank!'

Mum looked at the wall that separated us from the back guest room. I looked at the wall blankly.

'They're… you know… doing it,' Mum whispered.

'Doing it? Mum! That's a really common thing to say!' I was unsettled by this new version of my mother.

Mum's hands cupped her face and I watched her cheeks get redder as she stifled her laughter. Maybe she didn't care if things were common any more. Perhaps she was over all that kind of thing.

'It's not true, anyway,' I said.

My bones ached with the thought of Rita and Frank together. Rita must have got him very drunk. Why would he go and do it with her?

Soon Rita burst in, plonked herself down on the armchair and flounced her caftan, flapping up a breeze.

'Flippin' heck, I can't believe it, Brynn! I feel like I'm floating,' she said.

'You've covered in lovebites, Rita,' I said, trying to bring her smashing to the ground.

Rita's hand flew to her neck.

'He'll leather me!'

I spent ages combing out Rita's bites like I'd learnt to do years before, remembering Helen and her pet rat, and the first and only

192

time I'd been drunk, as I scraped the comb back and forth, so that the lovebites began to look like a natural rash. While I did this, Rita told me how she had gone all the way with Frank.

'He's a smashing lover, I can tell you that for nowt.'

After that I always avoided Frank. I no longer wanted him as my part-time dad.

*

Most of the guests were difficult to imagine as Dad types. Brian stayed for two nights and settled his bill, not with money – he didn't have any – but by painting Mum a large, glossy, orange sign with a yellow dandelion on it. He stuck it in the front garden on a large wooden stick. It stayed there until the council ordered it to be removed after complaints from neighbours. There was Horace, who hadn't paid a penny since the day he arrived. Mum said she was giving him the benefit of the doubt, but when his social security cheque finally came through, he just vanished without giving her any of it. Two plain-clothes policemen turned up looking for him, though they didn't say exactly why. I showed them Horace's room, which they searched. When they lifted his mattress, they found Mum's missing kitchen knives on top of a stack of porn magazines, which made me think I should maybe have a lock on my bedroom door. Mum didn't seem to take any of it seriously though, and laughed when she discovered where her knives had gone. She said she had no idea Horace was such a loony.

A proper lunatic did, in fact, stay in my room. Maybe he wasn't an actual lunatic, but he was definitely a schizophrenic. When he turned up, Mum made me give up my bedroom for him, as she had too many bookings. So I slept in the lounge with her, pondering over the life of the man who slept in my bed.

His name was Winston, and we knew he was a schizophrenic because his wife told us. 'It's just a temporary arrangement. I'm looking to buy us a house in another area,' she said. 'He's near his doctors here so it's better he doesn't come house-hunting with me. Winston won't be any trouble, he's drugged up to here,' she said, tapping her frazzled forehead.

When Winston's wife visited him, I would sit outside my bedroom door and listen. They didn't really have conversations, they had long silences, but even the silences fascinated me. I imagined the two of them sitting on my single bed holding hands.

Once I did hear them having a long conversation or, rather, she was talking a lot, about their children. She kept saying that she was sorry. So sorry. And I heard sobbing sounds, but I didn't know which one of them the sounds came from. She didn't come back to see him after that. All I could think about was his kids, and whether they would ever see him again and what it must be like to have a schizophrenic as a father. Mum had to contact social services eventually, as Winston's bill was no longer being paid.

'I guess she just couldn't take it any more,' Mum said. 'He was too much of a burden. It's hard living with a burden like that.'

I wondered if she was thinking of Dad, and if he had been a burden too. I was beginning to realise there were different kinds of mental problems. There was the visible kind and the invisible. Nobody could have guessed from looking at Dad what went on inside his head. He seemed perfectly normal from the outside. Perhaps it would have been better if he had looked on the outside like how he felt inside. It might have saved him. I would have looked at him and known then. Everybody would. He wouldn't have got a job, he wouldn't have had that car. If he was anything on the outside like he was on the inside he would have been put into intensive care or drugged up to the eyeballs, and watched over. At least he would have had a chance at life.

A van turned up and took Winston away. I wasn't there; Mum told me. But I imagined him leaving, his dark suit containing the vastness of his body. As he slowly descended the stairs with his heavy treads, I saw him focusing on something that nobody else could see, a nugget of life that still continued, somewhere in his brain, a memory of childhood, of running through a field of yellow corn, trying to catch up with the end of a rainbow.

brynn

There'd been so many jobs over the years she can't remember them all. She liked the one where she worked in a pub in Offerton. 'Hurry up please! It's time!' It had decent customers and she rode to work on a bicycle. What ever became of that bike? She can't remember. Where do things go? Where does time go?

Sometimes she feels a little guilty that her work meant that Ann especially was always getting foisted on people when she was little. In an emergency once, she even left her with the lollipop lady – though Ann loved being in her house and never stopped talking about the lollipop lady's counter in the kitchen, where she had sat on a stool and eaten her soup. She had let Ann enjoy talking about the counter, even though she herself thought that kitchen counters were very common.

She remembers the sharp face of the childminder Ann used to go to when she was three. Once, Ann woke up crying in the night and talked about being pushed onto a bed. When she tried to get to the bottom of it the childminder admitted that in the afternoons she went to bed for a sleep with all the kids, squeezed into her double bed. She finally stopped Ann going there when someone from work saw her in Stockport Market with all the other children the childminder looked after, all tied together with a rope, supposedly to keep them from straying.

There are some right characters out there, she thinks, smiling to herself. She ponders on the different types that have come and stayed at the guesthouse. If Ronald had been around he'd never've been up to running a place like this, that's for sure. He would have hated having people all around him, he would have seen it as a major aggravation. Sometimes she does too, but it comes with the job and somehow it keeps her going.

what branches grow?

'I'm a socialist,' I said.

'If I could put all my thirty-five years of knowledge in your fourteen-year-old head then you'd be a very clever little girl, that's what you'd be,' our head of year, Moonface, told me. Everybody called him Moonface because his face was round and cratered with acne scars and always seemed to be looming over us.

He looked down at my pink Jelly Baby sandals and fluorescent green ankle socks and sneered.

'What's this all about?' he asked, pointing at them.

'It's different,' I said, regretting what an unoriginal statement I'd made.

'Different?' he snorted.

'I'm not interested in being like other people,' I said, feeling lame.

'That's rich,' he said. 'If you were actually a true socialist you wouldn't give a flying hoot that you were like other people. In fact, you'd want to be.'

He brought his pent-up face too close to mine. I thought of Dad and his rage that seemed to come from nowhere.

'What do you say to that, hey?'

Moonface had a reputation for making girl pupils cry. Little did he know I hadn't cried for years and had no intention of doing so again, so he had no chance.

'Cat got your tongue?' he said.

He lifted the bow of the large, purple ribbon tied around my spiky hair.

'And what's this when it's at home?' he asked.

'A ribbon.'

'Don't go being sarcastic with me.'

'I wasn't being sarky. I was stating a fact.'

'Get it off. Now.'

I unravelled the ribbon. After that, Moonface ordered me to report to the deputy headmistress, Mrs Myers, each morning before the start of school so she could check what I was wearing. I knew Mrs Myers, as I was in her Personal and Social Development class. She talked about the Campaign for Nuclear Disarmament or venereal disease with equal passion, which shocked the entire class, considering her granny-like appearance. She was open to any kind of discussion, including rumours over whether Moonface was having an affair with the Art teacher. Much to the disbelief of my class, she exposed that this affair had indeed occurred, but was over, and that our head of year was back with his wife and children. I began to wonder if all fathers have affairs and, one way or another, leave their children.

The only teacher I admired was Mrs Pegg, my English teacher. She was strict and terrifying, but I found it a relief that she could control the unruly pupils that larked about the corridors and class-rooms, vying for attention. I once saw her slap a disruptive lad across the face in the cloakrooms and wanted to cheer. We all worked hard in her class to reach her high standards. When she told Mum at parents' evening that I was university material and that she would love to have me as a daughter, despite the fact that I dyed my hair, I felt like the chosen one. Because of Mrs Pegg, English was my favourite subject and I preferred reading to anything else. I became a regular at second-hand bookshops, preferring them to libraries as I could keep the books forever and write my name in the front and make notes in the margins.

Mrs Myers must have heard that I was doing well in English because she soon stopped bothering with what I was wearing and asked me what I was reading instead.

'Where are we this week then?'

Jude the Obscure,' I told her.

'Ah, I see,' she said, smiling. 'Read all you can!'

*

I didn't seem to thrive in my other classes though. In History the teacher returned my essay on the industrial revolution without a grade or any comments. I knew it was good, so that didn't seem right. After class I asked her why.

'Perhaps you could take some time to consider why the authors you copied have the opinions they do and have a think about why they think the way they do,' she said slowly, as though I was daft.

'But I didn't even look at a book! I just went off what we did in class. These are my ideas, honest Miss! Honest!'

I was mortified and could see she thought I was lying.

'I'm a socialist,' I said. 'I have left-wing leanings.'

'Oh,' she said, without listening or looking at me. 'I see.'

*

A series of Careers classes were given by Mr Twill, the Woodwork teacher.

'It's important to have clean nails when you go to an interview,' Mr Twill said.

I looked down at my broken fingernails, with the lines of dirt beneath them that only seemed to come clean when kneading pastry in Cookery class, and I wondered what age Dad had left school. I figured it was fourteen, because that was when people used to leave in the olden days, but I realised I didn't know for certain, and I didn't know if Dad had any qualifications either.

Mr Twill's dreary voice mentioned army training for the boys and secretarial courses for the girls. I thought of being asked what I wanted to do when I was a kid and telling people I wanted to be a scientist. I thought of all the types of jobs in the world and I realised that the kind of jobs Mum and Dad did were never the kind I heard people saying they wanted when they grew up. Our Maths teacher had recently told us we were the lucky generation, as our futures would be composed of leisure lifestyles, where we would all be paid handsomely for doing part-time jobs.

'And finally, just a last thought,' Mr Twill said, pausing for a while to torture us. Beneath his desk I noted, curiously, the ankle suspenders that held up his brown socks. 'If you work hard at your exams you might get a job. It's unlikely to be a job you want, but you might get a job.'

beat their wings

Mum spotted the clairvoyant's notice in the classified advertisements of the local paper, below the *Under a Fiver* section. He wanted a room to use one afternoon a week, as he was based in Oldham and some of his regular customers came from Stockport and found it quite a trek. Mum arranged for him to come round and look over our back room, which was the TV and dining room for the guests, and mostly unused in the daytime.

'Nothing bad has ever happened in this house,' said the clairvoyant, laying his hands on the woodchip wallpaper. 'This will suit me down to the ground.' His hair was black and slicked back, and he wore a dark suit. I half closed my eyes and his edges blurred, and for a split second Dad was there. The clairvoyant looked at me like I was strange in the head; or maybe he was looking at me like he had second sight.

'I'll read your palm for free one of these days, if you like,' he said.

'That'd be great,' I lied. I was thinking about fortune-tellers giving people nervous breakdowns by telling them too much about what lay ahead.

I stayed off school and faked a long telephone conversation so that I could monitor the women waiting for their consultations. They were all dressed in black and lined up on dining-room chairs that Mum had put against the wall in the hallway.

Could the clairvoyant really predict the future? I was sceptical. What were all these worried women looking for? What were they hoping to discover? Based on how miserable they all seemed, I imagined that they wanted to be told that their future was going to be happy. But would they really believe it? I doubted it. If people knew what was waiting for them in their futures, would they bother going on with their lives? What would be the point if there was nothing lined up but bad news and tragedy?

Could a fortune-teller have looked at Dad's palm when he was young and told him that he would have a wife, three children, and die by his own hand? Would there be any point knowing any of that? Could the future in our hands be changed if we wanted it to be? Or are we just born with lives ready to live out, like following a script? Was all my life already screwed up in my fist?

I looked at my palm and wondered if there was the line that marked the death of Dad. This was the point I decided that I really did want to find out what was waiting for me, whatever the outcome. The last of the clairvoyant's customers left and I knocked on his door.

'Come in.'

He was putting his tarot cards away. My nerves prickled and I wondered if I should go through with it. I took a deep breath and exhaled.

'Would yer read me palm?'

'Young lady, it would be my pleasure.'

He waved his hand at the chair opposite him and I sat down. He stared at me, as though he was reaching deep inside me, and I blushed. Even though I had only heard bad things about people who had their fortunes told, I felt oddly excited.

'Give me your left hand,' he said.

Nervously, I held it out.

'This is your lifeline.' He indicated with a point of his finger. 'This is your heartline and this is your headline.

'You're going to travel all over the world. People will be very jealous of you.'

Why were people going to be jealous of me? Maybe I truly was going to be a famous pop star and earn a fortune – I needed to get another band together.

He frowned. What was it?

'I see someone with black hair who finds you a negative influence in their life. They are themselves a negative force to be countered.'

I thought of who it could be, but drew a blank.

He looked at my palm again and an ambiguous look came to his face. He glanced at his watch.

'What is it?' I asked.

'I must get going,' he said. 'I didn't quite realise the time.'

My heart was pounding. Had he seen that I was to die soon? Was I going to get some disease? Did he know that I would be murdered? Had he seen how Dad had died and was embarrassed? Maybe he'd seen I was going to kill myself too?

Or maybe he hadn't seen anything at all.

*

The next week I saw Drac on the bus. I didn't hang out with her much any more, as her mum wouldn't let her go to gigs, but whenever I saw her I was always friendly and we'd talk about the latest music on John Peel's radio show and I'd tell her about the books I was reading and we'd reminisce and laugh about her mum's reaction to my choking on the fifty pence. Drac told me that her mum was planning to marry the tongue-and-groove boyfriend and that they were all moving to some grotty village somewhere nobody had ever heard of. We both bemoaned the fact we were too young to be in control of our lives and our futures. I told Drac about the clairvoyant and that I'd decided he was probably a fraud. He could no more see my future in the creases of my palm than I could. Then I told her he said someone with black hair was against me, and her face twitched uncontrollably. I looked at her black, spiky hair.

'He couldn't have meant you, right?' I said.

'Ann, I don't know how to say it but I have to be honest, right? I were tellin' someone yesterday that I hated yer. I'm dead sorry.'

She knitted her fingers together and cracked her knuckles, and I wondered if this was what was meant when writers described people as wringing their hands.

'Why do yer hate me?' I asked. 'Tell me, I won't mind.'

'Yer just don't seem real. That's what it is.'

'What do yer mean?'

'I dunno, really.' She shrugged.

'Do yer think I'm pretentious?' I asked. Being thought of as pretentious was my worst fear.

'Yeah summat like that,' she said. 'Yer always going on with these big words and everythin' and yer think you're a cut above everyone else.'

206

I was shocked. I thought of how I hated that Mum always thought we were better than other people. Now Drac thought I was exactly like my mum.

*

The clairvoyant never came back.

'He read Ann's palm and that was that, he was gone,' Mum said to Rita.

'Ann's a dark horse,' Rita said.

They both looked at me standing awkwardly in front of them and laughed. I began to understand why the ladies that had lined up to see the clairvoyant had looked so troubled. Finding out about your future was not a good thing at all. I wished that I had never let the clairvoyant look at my palm. It wasn't what he had said, it was what he hadn't said. It was how he had looked at me as though he had seen something bad. I began to think of the future not as a place to escape to, but as somewhere filled with bad things waiting to happen. The clairvoyant must have stopped coming to our house because he had seen something horrific lined up for me.

Mum and Rita recovered from their laughter attack.

'This one's as passive as anythin' in't she?' Rita said, looking me up and down.

'Oh she is, she really is,' Mum said, smiling and taking it as a compliment.

I rushed to my dictionary. Being passive meant I was lethargic and I had no interest. It seemed far worse than being pretentious. It was time to find love. That was going to be the best way out of being passive. I had turned fifteen and if I couldn't find love now then I doubted I ever would.

*

I met her at an Orange Juice gig. I say *her*, but she wanted me to call her *him*. Her last girlfriend had called her *he*, and her girlfriend's young son had called her Dad.

She was called Terry and was twenty-two and on the dole. She played the bass guitar.

'I nearly joined Bay City Rollers once,' she said. 'I got picked at the auditions. I were fifteen, your age.'

'So why din't yer join?'

'Me dad found out and phoned up the manager and told them I was a girl,' she said. 'He were always spoiling things.'

On the days I didn't see Terry she rang me from a phone box and wrote me letters. Mum knew that she was a girl but had no idea that we were going out together. If Queen Victoria didn't suspect that females could do sex things together, then I assumed neither would my mum.

When Mum got an extra booking, I would give up my bedroom and go and stay with Terry. Terry's flat was in a council tower block and I'm sure Mum would have found it common once, but she was too busy preparing breakfasts and dinners and making beds to be concerned whether things were common any more. Lots of people that visited the guesthouse were common by her old standards, but she didn't seem to mind.

*

Mum never gave me chores like characters in children's books were given, but I decided my regular chore would be to go to the launderette. Terry came with me once and we sat close together on the wooden slatted bench. I was becoming hypnotised by the spinning colours behind the bubbles of glass on the front of the washing machines.

'Where's yer dad?' Terry asked.

'He killed himself,' I said clearly. I felt nothing.

She looked at me, and I could almost hear the questions rustle about in her head.

'I nearly died once and it were quite nice,' Terry said. 'I were dying and I saw a light and I wanted to keep walking towards it. They say if yer reach it, yer dead.'

'Who do?'

'Oh, everyone and anyone that's nearly died has gone and said it.'

'How come yer nearly died?'

'It were raining dead hard. Me dad were driving and we were on the motorway and he overtook a big massive lorry and then he were skidding into fast lane and into a car. It were a miracle nobody died. I broke both me legs and I were out of it for a bit but I can remember the sound of me sister screaming and that's what stopped me going to that light. I don't know what it was. It weren't God, if that's what yer think I thought. I don't believe in him. If he existed he wouldn't have made me like I am.'

I squeezed Terry's hand quickly so that nobody would notice and she blew me a kiss.

'Are yer gonna show me a photo of your dad?'

'If yer like.'

There were two black and white photographs I kept in my dictionary – Dad's suicide letter was no longer there and I suspected Mum had discovered it and taken it back. There was one photograph with blurred, cloudy-white edges. In the background was an overgrown hedge. Dad was wearing tight dark jeans with a belt. He had on a white shirt and I was in his arms, an infant clutching his thin tie in my fingers. I had white hair and wore a white dress and

209

I was looking away from him, my mouth open, ready to cry. Dad's hair was as black and slicked back as ever, and he was looking at my open mouth.

Terry handed the photograph back. 'He's like Elvis,' she said, 'Elvis when he were young.'

'They died the same year,' I said.

I'd made a note of everyone in the news that had died in the same year as Dad. 'He died the same year as Elvis, Marc Bolan, Charlie Chaplin and Bing Crosby.'

I handed her the other small, square photograph. Dad wore a dark jacket, white shirt and pale tie. His arm was outstretched and his palm was flat against a brick wall. He was smiling but his eyes were shut and not letting me in. There was something about his closed eyes that really got to me, like he was already dead even then.

'He's a bit Gregory Peck in this one,' Terry said, handing the photo back.

No matter how hard I looked at the photographs I couldn't get rid of the thought that they were only bits of fragile paper. The photographs weren't enough. They weren't nearly enough. I put them back into my dictionary. I kept them amongst the *D* definitions. It seemed significant that there was only one letter difference between *Dad* and *Dead*.

*

'Can I take them something?' I asked Mum.

'You could cut up a couple of oranges and put them on a plate. That would do nicely, very refreshing,' Mum said.

I peeled the oranges and broke them apart, arranged them as petals and ran outside with the plate. The road swarmed thick and long with people marching, mostly men. They carried banners that showed a winding black road with a white line down the middle, which said *People's March For Jobs May '81 Liverpool–London*. I didn't know how many miles it was from Liverpool to London, but I reckoned it was hundreds, and they were going to walk it all – a real feat. I distributed the orange segments to the marchers.

'Good luck!' I said, as many times as I could.

Terry looked down at the people from the top of her ladder. Mum had got her painting the woodwork on the outside of the guesthouse. She looked longingly as the marchers passed and I wondered if she wanted to join them. She was registered unemployed after all.

*

Rita turned up later and said that Duncan and her had had a heated discussion over whether the person up the ladder was a boy or a girl.

'He said boy, but I said, no, he's too pretty to be a boy. It's got to be a girl.'

'He is a girl,' I said.

'I were right! That'll get him.'

Terry didn't want to be pretty. She wanted to be handsome. Around her chest there was a wide elastic bandage that kept her flat. She wouldn't remove the bandage or her Y-front underpants, so I never saw her naked body.

One night I reached between her legs, wanting to do what she did to me, but she pushed my hand away.

'Imagine yer were a bird and had no wings,' she said.

She told me how she'd visited a doctor and told him how she had been born into the wrong body.

'He laughed at me,' she said. 'He told me it were all in me head. I've written a poem about it.'

211

Besides wanting to be a man, Terry also wanted to be a poet. She had handmade business cards that said *Terry – Poet* with her address on them. She would leave piles of them in record companies and clubs but nobody ever wrote to request a poem, and some stacks of cards got sent back in the post. Her veiled poems always featured metaphors for being trapped.

*

'Let's go outside and see if we can see anything,' Terry said.

'But it's happening in Moss Side,' I said.

'It could spread, though,' Terry said, licking her lips.

We both wanted it to. We wanted to be a part of it. We had been watching the riots on the telly with growing anticipation. Buildings and cars were on fire, windows were being smashed, and there was violence and looting and petrol bombs and destruction and riot police barricades.

Terry stood outside the house with her hands on her narrow hips, looking up the stretch of main road.

'It's us and them,' Terry said.

As I expected, we couldn't see anything and so we went back inside to watch the TV. There was talk on the telly of bringing back the birch and of spraying people with gas.

'The law must be upheld, people must be protected,' Margaret Thatcher proclaimed.

'Bloody awful woman,' Mum said.

I realised how much Mum's opinions had changed since Dad had died. She'd never vote Conservative now.

We watched the riots spread on the television news. I sat with my chin propped in my hand and felt a thrill that all this was happening so close to us.

'Out of the ashes of these last days must come new life and hope,' commented some religious person on the TV.

'What's he witterin' on about?' Terry said, throwing an orange at the screen.

'These God types,' Mum said, 'they're just stuck in their ivory towers on their high horses, looking down at us. They haven't got a clue about real life.'

'You're not wrong there, Mrs Westbourne,' Terry said. 'The riots aren't just about race, y'know. When everyone left school in Liverpool recently there were only fifteen jobs available in the job centre. Everyone's told they should get a job but there ain't any bloody jobs to get. It's ludicrous. No wonder there's bleedin' riots.'

'Make us a cup of tea, go on Terry,' Mum said, smiling. 'There's a job for you.'

*

Terry came around to watch the royal wedding. We sat on dining-room chairs arranged in a circle around the TV. Terry and my sister sat either side of me, and the guests watched with us. Mum came in with a tray of cheese sandwiches cut into neat white triangles. What we were doing was what millions of people around the world were doing, watching Prince Charles and Lady Di get married. It felt as though I was on the same wavelength as the whole world for once.

We watched as Lady Di, her father beside her, shyly waved to the flag-waving crowds from her horse-drawn glass coach, which processed slowly through sunny London. Everyone was looking forward to Lady Di stepping out of the coach so that we could see her dress, which was rumoured to have the longest silk train a wedding dress had ever had. When we saw the dress, the biggest observation was that, considering the money that had been spent on it, it was terribly creased. It looked like she'd just taken it out of the launder-ette dryer.

'That dress could do with an iron,' said Susan, who had recently got engaged to Greg and had been given an ironing board by his sister as an engagement present.

'But she looks so beautiful,' said Alistair. He was our twenty-one-year-old Scottish guest. He had a black eye and a cut on his fore-head, crossed and hidden by pink plasters; he was accident-prone, he said, and had recently collided with a lamppost. In spite of his comment about Di, I knew he was really thinking how beautiful Susan was, because he kept casting her sidelong glances. Greg was missing the wedding celebrations, as he was in bed with flu, and I wondered what he would think about Alistair's interest in Susan. I concluded he'd probably punch him.

The TV camera switched from the flag-waving crowd to Diana inside the church, walking along a red carpet, holding her father's arm. I thought of how if I ever got married, I would never be given away by Dad wearing a grey suit and a white carnation in his buttonhole. I also thought about how unlikely it was I'd ever get married, and what a strange idea it was to be given away by your father. I looked at Susan, who had a faraway gaze in her eyes, and I wondered if she was absorbed in thoughts of Greg and her ironed wedding dress. Perhaps she was longing for the impossible – for Dad to give her away.

'Too young to get married is what I say,' Mum said. 'Mind you, I was already married at her age with a kid. But, then again, that was what people did in those days. No need for it now.'

We all laughed at Princess Margaret outside the church afterwards. Her arms were suspended in a strange position, like a puppet on a string, and the verdict was that she was drunk. But after that there was nothing much to report on. I grew impatient for something else to happen, so when Susan accepted Alistair's offer to take her for a ride somewhere in his Mini later that evening, I made sure that I was invited, and Terry too.

*

Susan sat in the front. Terry held my hand on the back seat, hidden from view.

'Where to?' Alistair asked.

'Alderley Edge,' said Susan.

'What's there?'

'The Edge,' said Terry, in a deep mysterious voice.

Alistair turned his headlights on into the fading light and pressed and accelerated onto the road. He was a chaotic driver and swerved and braked unexpectedly. Susan gave directions in a nervy whisper. I imagined her in the front, clutching onto her seat with fisted, white knuckles. Alistair pulled his handbrake up and the car screeched and turned the corner.

'Sorry,' said Alistair, grinning into the rear-view mirror.

His driving settled down and I relaxed and looked out of the window. Squares of house lights, beams of car headlamps and the low hanging, orange moon punctuated the press of bluish black, but even then there was a dark quality to the countryside that seemed threatening. My mind drifted to Lady Di earlier that day on television, and how a shot from above of her in her white dress made me think of the time I'd seen a swan landing on a pond.

A car came towards us out of the darkness on the other side of the road.

'He's way too young to be driving,' Susan said about the driver of the oncoming car, who looked younger than me.

'Bet it's nicked,' Terry said.

The car drew level and it was as though a flashbulb went off and froze the moment, because I saw the girl on the back seat so clearly and for much longer than was really possible. She was about my age but full of summer. She had freckles and sun-streaked hair, and her lower lip was swollen and expectant. She seemed fresh and uncomplicated, like I wanted to be. Her hand fluttered across the window, like the wing of a bird. She was waving at me.

We parked the Mini and shambled through the woods using a torch that Alistair had discovered under his seat. Alistair twisted his ankle in a hole and my sister let him lean on her shoulder for support. We reached the Edge, a jutting piece of ground with views of distant towns and their twinkling clusters of lights that Mum used to tell me were fairies. A dope-smoking hippy with long, lank hair had beaten us to it. He was sitting by a fire that he'd made. The flames flickered into the deep-purple night and sent glowing embers floating into the air as he told us he'd had a vision that we were coming. We shared his joint and exhaled the communal smoke into the warm night air.

I lay on my back and Terry lay beside me. Her body pressed secretly against mine. The hippy told us how there was a cave below us, where Arthur and his band of knights were frozen, waiting for the time when Britain needed them to return. On the damp, sandy earth, aware of laughter and the twisted smell of fire and smoke, I only half listened to the hippy spin tales of the wizard Merlin.

We stayed there till dawn, dozing, and woke shivering with cold as the fire had long since gone out. We said our goodbyes and promised the hippy that we'd all meet here on the same date and at the same time every year for the rest of our lives. We returned home happy, apart from Alistair. He was quiet and subdued, because he had discovered at some point in the drift of the night that Susan was engaged and his love for her was destined to be unrequited.

*

It was Alistair who pointed the story out to me in the newspaper, thrilled that it had happened on exactly the same night we had driven to Alderley Edge. A stolen car with four teenagers inside, driven by a fourteen-year-old boy, had crashed and overturned and all the passengers had been killed. I thought of the summery girl in the back of the car, her pale hand against the passenger window, waving at me, as clear to me that night as Lady Di had been in her glass carriage.

Two days later there was a solar eclipse, but according to the man on the television it was too far east to be seen from Britain. I wondered what it would be like though, seeing the full round moon wipe out the dagger rays of the sun and plunge the world into darkness.

brynn

She looks at the copy of his letter she discovered in Ann's dictionary some time ago. Each word stabs its way into her heart. Her eyes sting with tears as she reads.

Dear Brynn,

I'm so sorry to do this to you and the kids but since the last breakdown I just haven't felt right and I realise that I can't go on any more. I'm so sorry and I hope you will forgive me but I can't see any other way out. It feels like I've tried everything and nothing ever seems to work. I will only be a burden to you if I carry on. I hate to think I am leaving things in a terrible mess but they are only going to get worse if I am around. All I can ask is that you know that you are in no way to blame. I am so sorry to let you down.

All my love, Darling,

Ronald

Xxx

She folds his words up again and tries to put them from her mind, but she can't stop thinking of him. She decides to have a lie-down. She curls up on the settee, closes her eyes tight and wills herself into hollow, dreamless sleep.

the lady of situations

I went to school now and again, but never on Fridays. On Fridays I worked in the second-hand bookshop where my brother had once worked, and the owner seemed unaware that I was supposed to be at school. The bestselling books were the Mills and Boon romances and the Westerns, and there were some porn magazines that we shouldn't have been selling hidden away at the back that men would browse and sometimes buy, and I would put them into brown paper bags without making eye contact. But my favourite books were on a shelf near the window. I read Colette, Sylvia Plath, Dylan Thomas, Franz Kafka, Samuel Beckett and D. H. Lawrence, and the thrill of being a writer and the impossibility of matching their words came to me – I felt suffocated with hope and despair.

Even though I still loved Terry, I realised I needed my mind stimulated more, so I finished with her to go out with Terry's former flatmate, Janis, who was the cleverest woman I'd ever met. She was seventeen and stomped about in a man's suit, even though she didn't want to be a man, not like Terry did. Janis was anti lots of things, including beauty, and made no attempt to fit in with society's ideas of what a woman should look like, or behave like.

'I love being ugly,' she said. 'I like the way it gets up peoples' noses. Garrotte them all with their small, fucking narrow minds.'

Janis had gone to a grammar school but had to leave before her exams.

'I mean, all I did was wear pyjamas to school. The headmistress said to me: "I will not tolerate such acts of disrespect. Please leave these premises and never return to darken our doorstep." I think what really got to her was that I had the audacity to turn up in *men's* pyjamas.'

Janis didn't have a dad around, but she never told me why, and I knew not to ask questions after my first few ones, as she had put an invisible wall up where enquiries about him were concerned. She had left home at sixteen and now she was signed on the dole and had ambitions to be a proper writer, and began to encourage me to write more than my occasional sentences so that we could go and live in Paris together and write for a living.

'I want us to be a notorious couple,' Janis said. 'Not a gay couple, no – we would be like Sartre and de Beauvoir. A force times two.'

She gave me a reading list and books that included *The Catcher in the Rye*, *The Outsider* and *La Bâtarde*. She wrote down page numbers that I should pay particular attention to and we lay about in bed a lot, talking about literature and our relationship.

'I can't understand what you see in me but I adore you,' Janis said. Her face was softer than the one she used on the street. 'Don't feel awful about having someone think you're wonderful, it's one of the best things in the world. I want to be your slave! Does that scare you? It scares me! I hope you don't just go out with me because I'm kind and dependable,' she said.

'Course not,' I replied, knowing it was her mind that had seduced me.

Janis lay on her front and pushed her face into her pillow. I sat on her fleshy bum and scratched satisfying lines of blood to the surface of her back.

'Sartre, y'know, thought suicide was a way of responding to how absurd life was,' she said, her voice muffled. 'He saw suicide as a logical reaction to life.'

Was what Dad did just a logical reaction to life? In so many ways, I could see his point.

'But Camus, right, saw it differently,' Janis continued. 'He saw suicide as a kind of weakness. He thought that if you killed yourself you weren't up to facing life as what it really is. Nothing. Life is nothing.'

I looked at the scrapings of Janice's skin under my jagged nails and felt panic.

'But life's got to be something,' I said.

'Does it? Most people go and get married, have kids and nine-to-five jobs and get up day after day and do the same thing. Then their children grow up and do it all over again. Even if we don't do that – what's the point of it all anyway?'

Anger surged inside me. It was too hard to bear to think of life amounting to nothing. Then a thought came to me.

'What about love?' I asked.

'Aren't you the romantic,' she said, as she roughly pushed me off her back, turned on her side and lifted my skirt. 'Does love really mean anything in the scheme of things?' she said, looking into my eyes and burrowing her fingers deep inside of me.

'But isn't love the point?' I said.

I thought about Dad not being able to face up to life being nothing at all. Maybe if he had known just how much I loved him he would have stayed around – why didn't I kiss him that last time I saw him? But if life really was nothing then maybe it didn't matter that he had gone and done himself in. Maybe it just didn't matter at all.

'And I read somewhere,' Janis said, 'though I forget who it was that wrote it, that to kill yourself is to destroy the world.'

I closed my eyes and tried to close my ears. I no longer wanted to hear any more of Janis' quotes.

*

'Ann! Get down here now!' Mum shouted in my dream. She was looking up at me on the top of a mountain and watching me about to jump. I woke up and realised that Mum was calling me in real life. I got up and threw on my clothes, rushed downstairs and prayed with each step that nothing had happened. Mum was at the front door, holding it open a few inches. I thought of the policeman and policewoman knocking us awake all those years ago.

'Here she is,' Mum said.

She opened the door wider to present me and I saw a woman behind a clipboard with eyebrows plucked into a surprised expression. I realised with dull dread that this was the truant officer.

'She's been working away on her studies at home, haven't you?' Mum said. She was using the posh voice she used for the telephone, debt collectors and authority figures of any kind.

The officer tried to edge her way inside, but Mum narrowed the door a fraction.

'She hasn't been well.'

'What's the matter with her?' the officer said, peering over Mum's shoulder at me.

'Oh, flu and things, isn't that right, Ann?'

I nodded. The officer scanned her clipboard.

'That doesn't account for all these missing weeks and days, though, does it, Mrs Westbourne?'

School was so noisy and chaotic and fraught with tensions that I never wanted to go. If people were there to learn I would maybe have gone, but that was the last thing on most minds and nobody at all ever talked about anything transformational. Even the Art classes got out of hand, with paint being thrown about the room, and not in a Jackson Pollock kind of way. The only classes I ever attended were English classes with Mrs Pegg.

'It's likely you'll be prosecuted. This matter will be going to the town hall,' the officer told Mum.

'That's a help,' Mum said in her driest tone.

The officer lifted her arch eyebrows and looked at me. 'Don't you want to take exams and get on?'

'Oh, she's taking examinations, aren't you, Ann?' Mum said.

'GCEs in English Language, English Literature and Art, and five CSEs,' I said, wishing I could say eight GCEs, which would have sounded much better.

The officer raised a single eyebrow, which I took to be a sign that she was surprised I was even sitting any exams.

'She's likely to pass them too, the amount of work she puts in,' Mum said.

The officer looked at Mum.

'I would advise you to make sure she comes to school, Mrs Westbourne.'

'I'm on the case.'

Mum shut the door firmly and leaned her back against it with a smile of triumph. 'Haughty cow,' she said.

*

I went out with Janis for a few months, and it was educational in many ways. Not only did she widen my knowledge of authors, she took me to my first lesbian-and-gay bar near Manchester coach station. I picked at the black nail varnish on my fingers and looked around, wishing I fitted in. When and where was I ever going to feel like I belonged? I realised then that I didn't belong with Janis either. I finished with her but couldn't explain why, which made her angry. I wanted to tell her that I was finding it hard to feel anything at all about anything at all, but I didn't know how. For all the books I was reading, I didn't seem able to use words properly.

'You're so disconnected, Ann, you really are. You haven't got a clue, you just treat everyone like an extra in a movie that you're the star of,' Janis said.

She was right. I did feel like I was in a movie. I was in a movie that wasn't moving and I was frozen. I didn't know where to go any more, or how to get there.

*

A few weeks after finishing with Janis, I had completed her reading list and I was now choosing my own books. It was the middle of the night and I was reading Saki by torchlight, lying on settee cushions on the floor in the front room as Mum had rented my bedroom out for a few nights. I finished one of his short stories, about a missing woman who returned to her family after eight years and I wished that Dad could come back, that it had all been a mistake. I listened to the lorries hurtling along outside, heading somewhere else, and I wondered about where I was going, where all this would end. In the darkness I hoped that I could disappear and I didn't want to wait for the moment, or to come back.

'Take me,' I whispered to the universe. 'Please take me.'

'What's that?' Mum said, groggy from disturbed sleep.

'Nothing,' I said, as I wished even harder for oblivion.

lost bones

'Tell us you'll read it,' they said, pressing the book into my hands.

'Yeah, all right, I promise,' I said. Brenda and Bill were a married couple of Jehovah's Witnesses who always dressed alike in beige and were staying in the bedroom next to mine.

'Oh good,' they said in unison, beaming.

They said it was a book especially written for 'young people'. When I looked at it later, I found a chapter on the evils of masturbation. I wondered if Brenda and Bill had seen into my bedroom. I discarded the book and went to bed.

Under my quilt I decided that I was not immoral, but amoral. I was, to quote my dictionary, *outside the domain of morality* and I realised I was probably like Meursault in *The Outsider*. After all, Meursault never cried for his mother when she died, and I had never cried for Dad.

Inside of me there was a dark weight. It seemed more real than the sensation of being hungry or sick. It made happiness seem like a con. This was the real thing. It was gripping and it gripped me. This was what life really felt like. I wanted to become a fossil that would be discovered in a million years' time, all hard and set in stone. I wanted to put black rubbish bags over my window to cut out the light and barricade my bedroom door but I was too tired to bother. Instead I spent a few days sleeping, cutting out the light with my eyelids, making late-night visits to the toilet, returning to dreams full of faces, stretched out in front of me like demons, fingers wagging, sending me into shadowy, murderous corners to discover my victims.

When I finally did get up, which wasn't a conscious decision but instead felt like my body was dragging me, I was light-headed and the edges of objects glowed and appeared unreal, fizzing out into the air. The house was quiet, and I found Mum in the front room, pretending to be asleep on the settee. Beside her there was a screwed up letter, which I picked up and smoothed out. My eyes began to focus and I saw it was the council informing her that, after an annual inspection, Dandelion Guest House had failed to meet fire regulations and was to be closed down with immediate effect.

Mum stopped faking being asleep and scratched at the raw patch of psoriasis on her elbow. 'I had my hopes pinned to this place,' she said. 'What are we going to do now?'

*

After a week, Mum's fighting spirit returned and she said she was not going to let the council's high and mighty get the better of her. She decided that she would turn the house into a shared house, which meant she didn't have to declare to the council that she had tenants and so she wouldn't have to adhere to regulations, such as fire doors, which only the rich could possibly afford.

'We'll rent out your bedroom and you'll come in the lounge with me,' she said.

I buried my gloomy feelings that I was about to be without a bedroom again, but sighed loudly to make sure Mum knew the arrangement was far from ideal.

'It won't be for long, Ann. We'll get ourselves a little place of our own after a bit. I swear we will. Maybe we could convert the cellar here into our very own flat.'

My sixteenth birthday was not too far away and, even though it was horribly old, it offered me some consolation. It meant that in a few months I could leave school. I could leave home. I would be able to get away from everything, though at the back of my mind there was the worrying thought of how Mum would cope without me.

Mum's advert in the local paper soon brought a group of people to live with us. 'Young twenty-something working professionals,' Mum said, clapping her hands together.

Peter worked at the McVitie's factory and brought home boxes of reject biscuits for everyone to share. Valerie waited in every night hoping her married boyfriend would ring. Philip, who took my room, had an inherited eye condition that meant he would eventually go blind, and there was Celia, who worked for an insurance company and caught me snooping about her room.

'What the hell are you doing in here?' Celia shouted.

But I couldn't really explain. I often looked through all their bedrooms, to try and get a feel for how other people lived. I wanted to tell her that I wanted to crawl inside of her, because that's what I really wanted to do, to move into someone's body and mind for a while, to see what they saw, to think what they thought, to try and compare and discover if my life was really strange or wrong. But that sounded really weird and I knew I was better off saying nothing at all.

'I have every intention of putting a lock on my door,' Celia said, though she never did.

Last to arrive was Barry, a civil servant from Northern Ireland, who said he was on a civil service scheme for workers to leave Northern Ireland for a year to get away from the Troubles and experience peace. Poor Barry. Of all the places he could have gone to, I pitied him being landed with Stockport. He seemed happy enough though. He was always whistling and cheerfully did the piles of washing-up that everyone else left.

I was eating a misshapen biscuit and watching the local news on the telly when I first heard of the Falklands. I considered myself a pacifist, but secretly I longed for a war. I had read the war poets at school and I knew about *the pity of war*, but there was still a part of me that wanted to live through conflict. Lots of lads in town had once had their hair shaved to be extras in *Yanks*, a film shot around our way. I had seen the film and it made me think that war had its good side. I wanted to hide in air-raid shelters and sing songs with neighbours and wave goodbye to the troops and make do and mend. I thought it would be fun to paint my legs with tea and draw black lines up the back to resemble stockings. We would have street parties to celebrate our victory.

The war seemed to happen elsewhere though. There were no aircraft overhead, no air-raid sirens, no bombs and no GIs bringing chewing gum from America, not that we needed any, we seemed to have plenty of our own stuck to the pavement. The togetherness I was hoping for never happened.

What was the point of a war if it never happened around where you lived? I wanted to see the sky lit up with a falling bomb. I wanted to discover how brave I could be and crawl through the rubble looking for survivors. I wanted to imagine Dad bravely fighting on the front – though he'd probably be old enough now to be in the Dad's Army; but there didn't seem to be one of those either.

'Northern Ireland is staying neutral on the Falklands,' Barry told me, which seemed sensible, seeing as it was a daft kind of war.

'It all comes down to land ownership,' Barry continued. 'It's nothing like the Second World War. Now that was a war that needed to be fought; it was a war to stop Hitler.'

But when men from both sides started dying in the Falklands I was ashamed that I had ever wished for it to happen. Some of the soldiers from the Cheshire Regiment had gone to my school. They were lost now, gone forever, they had no choices about life any more, or death. War really was closer to home than I'd thought.

*

I had finished my mock English Literature exam and was hiding from everyone in a toilet cubicle, deciding to wait until the crowds had died down to emerge. Once it sounded quiet, I came out to find Jilly waiting for me. I felt the slow creep of old fear and tried to snuff it out. I gripped my insides and the memory of that yellow letter at primary school. It was like a poem that I'd been made to learn off by heart.

'I wanted to tell yer summat,' she said.

She was about to mess with my head but at the same time as feeling ancient doom, I was also intrigued that after all this time she still had it in for me. Her face was the same, pretty and framed by her strawberry blond hair. Her chest was flat. I had changed so much. What I hadn't changed myself with make-up and haircuts and hair dye, my body had finished for me. The only thing different about Jilly was that she was taller and not as cocky. She looked sheepishly down at the concrete floor like she had something to be ashamed about.

'The thing is… I wanted to tell yer…' she trailed off. 'I thought yer should know…'

She looked down at her shoes.

'Me sister's husband…' she said.

What was it? What did her sister's husband have to do with me? I felt like I was watching an episode of *Coronation Street* unfold.

Jilly watched herself knock the metal tips of her scuffed granny shoes together, like she was Dorothy in *The Wizard of Oz* trying to get out of Kansas. Or trying to get back there. I waited.

She looked at me and took an intake of breath and quickly exhaled her words.

'Yer see, I thought yer should know, me brother-in-law done what your dad did in 'is car.'

'In his car?' I repeated, realising I sounded moronic and posh, which was the last thing I wanted to seem in front of Jilly. Luckily, she didn't appear to notice. I wondered how she knew how Dad had actually died. Who had told her?

'Me sister wanted a divorce but Tim couldn't cope or summat like that. She's dead upset, obviously.'

It was a connection after all this time but it all seemed too late. Jilly's bad news wasn't my news.

'I'm sorry,' I said, uselessly.

'I just thought yer should know, that's all,' Jilly said.

She fiddled with her gold ear stud and watched me. The words slowly formed on my lips.

'How did yer know how me dad died?'

Jilly released the ball of her earring.

'It were in local paper – me sister saw it at the time.'

I'd not seen it in the paper, and hearing it now felt like I had just found out about Dad dying all over again. I felt humiliated and my cheeks reddened. I rushed into a toilet cubicle and bolted the door.

I heard Jilly scuffling her feet on the other side of the door and imagined thrusting her head down a dirty toilet and pulling the chain.

She knocked on the door.

'All right?'

'Yeah, I'm fine ta.'

'Well I better be getting off… See yer then.'

I sat on the toilet and put my hands out in front of me. They were trembling. I placed them underneath my thighs and sat on them. Dad had died five years ago. Why did it only seem like yesterday? It was so long ago – why had I not got over it? I was different then. He wouldn't recognise me if he came back, that child he knew was gone – inside and out. He would be disappointed and he'd think I was common. I knew that for sure. I only existed like I did because he did not. If someone cut me open and sawed through any one of my bones they would find a ring, like the rings trees had to show their age, but my ring would be thick and black and mark the time Dad had gone and disappeared.

For years, Jilly had felt like the enemy. Someone who went through life sneering at people, with nothing in her heart. But now she and I were even because someone close to her had done what Dad did. Now she knew how it felt to have no answers. But it was all too late.

I thought about her yellow letter. The words linked to Dad and to everything bad I had ever felt. I knew that I would never forget it for the rest of my life. It was crawling around inside of me, ready to bite. It bit me in my dreams and in my waking hours, and it followed me everywhere. All the letters did. Dad's suicide letter, with its photocopied creases and folds, his last words – even though they made no mention of me. The letter Mum had told me that the Granddad I had never met had written to Dad asking to see him. The letter for me, from Grandma Westbourne, for when I was married. Did these letters explain anything? Would Grandma's letter provide an explanation for everything, for what she had done to Dad? I knew somehow that I would never see that letter, that I would never get married and have children, that I was never going to be able to live my life like that.

I opened my eyes and focused on the graffiti scrawled on the door in front of me. Amongst the swear words and leery rhymes, it was mostly names, a stab at telling the world that they had existed. Under the peeling yellowing paint, there were other names being called. There were other names under there, a whole history.

brynn

The newspaper cutting from the *Stockport Advertiser* is yellowed with age, almost brittle, as she unfolds it now. She remembers cutting it out, thinking of all the people who had seen it, who knew her business, and how ashamed she had been. She reads it again:

LOCAL MAN - INQUEST

A Stockport man, who was found in his car with a length of rubber pipe running from the exhaust pipe into the vehicle, died of carbon monoxide poisoning, an inquest held at Slough Guildhall Coroner's Court heard. Ronald Westbourne, 40, of Oak Grove, Heaton Moor, who was married with three children, was discovered in a secluded lane by a passing couple walking their dog. A letter found in the car, said the coroner, was of a private nature but 'convinced me that he was suffering from acute depression.' The inquest heard that Mr Westbourne had a history of depression and that at the time of his death the balance of his mind was disturbed.

What about the balance of her own mind? Would electric shock treatments give her some kind of relief? It had never helped him though, so it's probably a ridiculous idea. She decides she no longer wants to keep the newspaper cutting. She folds it into a tiny square, holds it tight in her hand and feels the sharp edges dig into her palm. But she doesn't let go.

da da da

'I spent a whole hour driving around looking for you,' said my Geography teacher, Mrs Green. She had trapped me in the corridor on the way to my English Literature exam, furious that I had not turned up for my Geography exam. 'If you'd taken it, Ann, you may well have managed a grade-one CSE,' she said. I didn't tell her that I looked down on CSEs as qualifications and therefore they meant nothing to me. I merely shrugged. In return, she was enraged by my apparent lack of interest.

'Don't you want to make something of yourself?' Mrs Green asked.

'I want to make hats,' I told her. 'I want to be a famous milliner.'

The hat idea had only come to me a few days before. I had no real concept of what making hats involved, or if you really could get famous making them.

'Well I suppose you would be following in Stockport history, as it was once a hat manufacturing town of great repute,' Mrs Green said. 'Even so, without qualifications you'll have a tough time getting anywhere, young lady.'

*

Something happened in Manchester at this time that made school, teachers and exams fade completely into the background. The Haçienda nightclub opened for the first time. It was named after the Spanish word for home. It became mine.

The Haçienda was a vast, industrial-styled space that was often underpopulated, but downstairs was a small cocktail bar named the Gay Traitor, apparently after the British spy Anthony Blunt. This was where everyone congregated for warmth. In the first week it opened I started off drinking Pernod and black, and by the end of the week I was drinking whisky. I hadn't drunk for four years, and I wondered why not, because it made me confident, strong and witty. It also gave me the urge to sleep with almost every person I spoke to.

At the end of the second week of my regular attendance at the Haçienda, fuelled by whisky, I met a lad who described me as 'very excitable', and I decided he would be the one I would lose my virginity to. I made it impossible for him to decline and he left the club with me clasped to his side, staggering like a three-legged race back towards Hulme Crescents, where he lived. He talked of streets in the sky and how every block of flats in Hulme was named after an architect.

The thrill of booze is that you get black holes; whole pieces of a puzzle go missing. The bits I remember of that night are disjointed but strong. Fragments of conversation and places and feelings. I remember an underpass with walls covered in graffiti, which looked too neat.

'I bet if this were a play on telly you'd say it weren't what real graffiti looked like,' I said to the lad. I'm not sure if he replied.

I was in a bedroom stretched out on a mattress on the floor.

'Don't wanna get you pregnant,' I remember he said, opening a drawer and taking out a condom.

My dress was pushed up to my thighs and then he was on top of me, pumping away. Through his window I counted the lighted squares of windows outside and there were a lot, probably because hardly anyone in Hulme had a job to get up for.

My first time with a boy. I closed my eyes and wondered if his body inside mine would make me understand him or other people. Was he thinking? I didn't think so. He seemed like an animal, thrusting motion into me. I thought that this was how life came about. If it wasn't for the condom I could have had a baby, a little life of my own. The possibility of something growing inside and taking me over, the strange thought of that. A dull pain, a dull ache in my head, between my legs, I wondered if there was any booze anywhere, another drink.

He rolled from me and lit a cigarette and blew out smoke into the chilly air. I held his soft cock in my hand. I kept reminding myself that this was an important moment, and I should have something to remember it by, something solid. Later, when he was looking around for something to drink, I looked at his sheets, hoping to find virgin blood. I wanted to cut it from the sheet and keep it forever, but there wasn't any blood and I felt cheated.

The next day when we woke up he put his fingers inside of me and measured me up. He told me his name was Jay.

Jay was a handsome university drop-out with a strong jawline and jet black, wavy hair. He'd given up his architecture degree,

241

preferring the Haçienda to studying. We began to see each other and, because he was on the dole and broke most of the time, he seemed to owe money to everyone he knew, crossing roads and hiding in dark corners to avoid them. I spent most of my time thinking about Jay. I was always thinking about places we could do it, and how I would do it to him. I had graduated from laying flat as an envelope underneath him, to a variety of positions. One extended night Jay had seven orgasms and he notched each one into his wooden headboard with a penknife.

Jay said that we should have sex in the bath, that it was the greatest thing in the world. The problem was that he shared the bathroom with other people and it was hard to ever get much time in my bathroom at home, what with all the tenants. So we never did try it. We had sex where we could though – in his bed, in my bed, outside and, once, in the Haçienda, on the balcony that jutted out over the cocktail bar.

Jay taught me the rules of cricket and told me that Samuel Beckett had said that in cricket the whole of life was played out. I thought back to my teacher Mrs Finzi in junior school and how much she had loved cricket, and I tried to work out how cricket rules applied to life. I listened to the game on the radio and noted down the results on a special score sheet Jay kept. *Maiden over, wrong-footed, all-rounder, follow through, innings, sticky wicket, leg bye, dead ball, fast bowling, the run-up, run out, slider, back foot, point of release.*

After we had been seeing each other a couple of months, I assumed that what I had with Jay was real, a relationship to keep hold of. I told him with a hopeful smile that he'd most definitely bowled me over and I asked him if I could move in with him, but he shifted about uneasily before he came up with an answer.

'It was a good innings while it lasted, but I'm just a tease, remember?'

And that was that, we were over and, to use one of his crass cricket expressions, I was stumped.

*

School was over too and the prosecution against Mum for my truanting had taken too long to go through the system and was dropped. Mum got us both new jobs working for an international market research company.

Our first assignment was referred to as 'in the field'. I thought a better name would have been 'in the street' as that was where we had to stop people. Armed with a clipboard and sheets of questionnaires, I approached strangers and asked them to come up to a room with me to try out a new kind of dissolving aspirin. In return they would get a free Mars Bar.

When we reached our target, the supervisor bought us all cream cakes. We sat around the room and I listened to the talk of nappies and teething and children's illnesses – wondering why it was only women who did this kind of job. Mum joined in and I wondered if this was it, this was my life.

'Ann had to have grommets in her ears when she was little,' Mum said. 'She was as deaf as a post before that. It's an issue of catarrh.'

When she talked like this, Mum made our life together sound normal, when it was anything but in my mind. I always thought that the only time things had ever felt normal to me was when Dad was alive. But I knew that life hadn't been normal then either. I was mistaking being a conventional family for being normal. Gripping the edge of my plastic clipboard, I bowed it in my hands. Mum was eating a cake, and I watched critically as she licked the cream from around her lips. I was not eating cake. I did not want to get fat like her.

My brother had recently interviewed Martin Fry, the lead singer from ABC, and he had said that the most important thing you needed to get you where you wanted to be was the power of the imagination. I decided I had no imagination. After all, why else was I in a dead-end job in Stockport pushing aspirins onto un-witting passers-by?

Maybe I was destined to work in a factory for the rest of my life or, as my mum lamely joked, maybe I would end up behind the coun-ter at Woolworth's. I wasn't much good at anything. Not school, not music. I didn't know how to play an instrument properly and I was definitely too old to learn. When I had been going out with Janis and she had told me to write, I had been too scared to show myself up, unable to express all the thoughts and feelings that raged inside of me like poison arrows. I was useless; so how on earth was I going to get away from all this? It was dawning on me that just because you wanted something to happen, it was not necessarily going to, even if you spent large parts of your life imagining it, as Martin Fry suggested. I was stuck.

Instead of worrying about my damned future, I put all my efforts into going to the Haçienda. In order to hang out there on a regu-lar basis, I decided I needed something to bolster my confidence, something unforgettable and interesting. I went to a toy shop and bought a battery-powered train set, a hobby-horse and, inspired by the inclusion of a duck in a Sylvia Plath poem, I bought a yellow duck on a stick with wheels. I set up the train set on the counter of the cocktail bar, and my duck or horse was always at my side like a comedy partner. Drinking made me feel as sparkly as Dorothy

244

Parker as I made acidic comments until my tongue began to snake into some stranger's mouth.

'You're incorrigible,' said the barmaid. I made her write the word down for me and when I found the scrap of paper in my bag sometime later, I looked it up in my dictionary: *Beyond correction or reform*. I liked that. The idea of being beyond anything was interesting. Very interesting.

The main things on my mind when I got down to the club every night, was who I could have an intelligent conversation with and who I would shag. Boy or girl. It felt like power, as though I could own the world that way. I especially liked it when I hooked an important person – someone that managed a band, or was in a band, or who ran a record label. I hoped that a little bit of them would rub off on me.

Often I would wake up with people that I didn't remember meeting the night before, and other times I would find myself curled up alone in a shop doorway, my mind heavy and pitted. Once I woke up upright in a cupboard, a curve of a wire coat hanger poking into my back and a sliver of memory of the fattest woman I had ever seen with my fingers inside of her.

I began to wonder what all the fuss was about women charging for sex. Why was it such a bad thing to do? It was something I decided I was good at, so it would be an easy way to make money.

One thing I was sure of. Alcohol was the best thing that had ever happened to me.

Things happen. Memories ease up and slip away.

Once, I overheard Mum say that Dad never drank because he was afraid that he might never stop, that he might become an alcoholic.

But perhaps it could have saved his life.

It might have stripped his nerves right off.

*

Even though I was getting drunk as much as possible and hoping to meet someone who would make me famous, I was still looking for other ways to get a different life. I enrolled at Rochdale College of Art to do a pre-foundation course and an A-level in Art History. I wasn't sure why I wanted to do Art, but it was something you could study without qualifications, so was somewhere to go. I'd chosen Rochdale over Stockport College, because soon after Ian Curtis died the remaining members of Joy Division had played a gig at Rochdale College before going on to name themselves New Order. Rochdale felt the right place to be, even though it was over an hour away on the bus.

In an Art History lesson we were asked to write about the Dada movement for twenty minutes. Everyone around me moaned that they had never heard of Dada and had no idea what to write.

'Write anything that comes into your head,' Pam, the teacher who insisted we called by her first name, said.

Luckily, Dada was something I had heard about. Thanks to Gordon, the barman from the Haçienda cocktail bar who had an Art degree, I knew it was the French word for hobby-horse as well as an art movement originating in Zurich. I recalled everything Gordon had told me as I wrote about anti-art, and Marcel Duchamp and the horrors of the First World War that the Dadaists were reacting to. I felt sure Pam would end up reading what I had written out loud to the class. I was the only one that seemed to be writing very much and it wouldn't be the first time my work had been read out loud by a teacher. In my first year at secondary school my English teacher had read my story to the class. It was about a girl of my age, living next door to an old man who she had become friends with, who'd won the pools. He died and left the girl his pool winnings, but she didn't care, as all she wanted was the man back. There'd been a few sniggers from a particular boy in the class, and all in all it was a humiliating experience. I put that story to the back of my mind, sure that this time my words would be met with nothing but admiration.

Pam collected our work and returned to her desk. She tore all our pages into pieces and threw them into the bin.

'There you go. That's Dada,' she said.

I'd only been at college a few months, but I left after that lesson and took up permanent residence again at the Haçienda, where things still made more sense to me than anywhere else. I was always welcome there. The doormen let me sneak in for free and I managed somehow never to pay for a drink.

One night in the cocktail bar, I was drinking something called Death in the Afternoon that Gordon the barman had given me and began an argument with a woman about Ian Curtis. She was claiming that Ian's suicide was a cowardly way out.

'But it's heroic!' I shouted. 'It's a brave thing to do.'

Even though at other times I wasn't sure, at that moment I believed without a doubt that suicide was brave. I wasn't having anything said against Dad.

'That's ludicrous,' she said. 'Why go around romanticising something so weak and stupid?'

The thought of my father being weak and stupid made me so angry that I threw my cocktail in her face, watching as it slapped her, for a second forming a watery, glassy veil. People around us stopped and looked and didn't bother to whisper what they thought.

'Fucking nightmare that girl.'

'She should be barred.'

'She'll come to grief.'

Fuck her, fuck them, I thought. I'm not getting barred. The only person who'd ever been barred from the Haçienda was one of the owners' dads, who'd stripped naked and tried to have sex with a bollard that was used to section off the dance floor.

Instead, I headed for the upstairs bar, the argument still raging in my head. Why had I not been more articulate and said that life was all that we had and we could either see it as a curse or a blessing or somewhere in between, but our lives were ours to do what we wanted with? Why hadn't I said that killing yourself was not an act of cowardice but of common sense?

At the top of the stairs I stumbled into the bar manager, Sam. He was forty-two, married with kids, did weight lifting as a hobby, and always gave me free drinks.

'Hello Smiley,' he said.

I felt terrible, but I grinned, not wanting to let him down.

'Fancy a private tour? Behind the scenes of the Hac and all that?' he asked.

As Sam showed me around the dressing rooms and the offices and the empty spaces that he said had been used for building boats, I began to consider how I would kill myself. I was certain I would one day, it was just a matter of when. I had not worked up the guts to do it yet. To me, this proved that it wasn't a cowardly act, not if you needed so much courage to do it.

But what was really stopping me was not knowing what happened afterwards, after you'd done it. I'd got it into my head that the way you feel when you kill yourself, which must be terrible, obviously, was the mood that would stay with you throughout eternity, if eternity did exist. I had a sneaking suspicion that all the suicides of history were writhing around on some astral plane, in a state of limbo, their minds still tortured by what had made them take their own lives in the first place.

Was Dad in that awful state of limbo? I hated to think of him caught, on an incomplete journey, endlessly feeling the same pain. I didn't want to think that he was being punished, but I couldn't help thinking, well, maybe he was. There was no way of knowing until you did it yourself, and I couldn't face taking that risk yet.

Sam shone his torch into a dank, airless room and led me across it. I could feel water under my feet. We reached a dry part of the floor, and then he did what seemed to be inevitable these days with men and me. It was what I'd taken to doing without a thought, but right now I didn't want to. Sam took his jacket off and laid it on the ground and placed the torch upright next to it. He circled his arms around me, pulled me close and kissed me, his full lips overlapping mine. I dropped my hobby-horse and listened to it clatter and bounce on the concrete floor.

He pulled me down next to him. He fumbled with his zip and I heard the rip of a condom packet. He pushed my dress up and my knickers down. He was on top of me and inside me. I wished I was drunker. I watched the focused white light from the torch, hard circles spilling out on the ceiling, and imagined that it was the tunnel of light I was going to see on my death. I let him do it to me even though I didn't want to; it was better than letting him down. It was something I could be useful for. Some kind of purpose. I wondered if he was disappointed that I was quiet and still. He groaned and gave his last thrust.

'Okay, Smiley?' Sam asked.

I smiled.

Afterwards he led me back to the cocktail bar and took a full bottle of whisky from behind the counter and gave it to me like an award. The woman who I had thrown a drink at had gone and I wished that she was there to see that I was being presented with free booze. I unscrewed the metal lid and poured the amber heat into my mouth straight from the bottle and dived into the blackness.

*

From the moment you are born, I realised, you start to die, but from the moment that I turned sixteen I could actually feel myself dying. I knew now that I wanted to leave this world I was in more than anything else. I bought some aspirin. The instructions on the packet said not to take more than eight tablets in a day. I managed fifteen in one go, but I couldn't swallow any more. Whatever it took, I did not have it in me.

Later I vomited strange, bright green strings of bile. I made my mind up that the next time that I tried to kill myself it wouldn't be with pills. They were too hard to swallow. I thought of all the ways that you could kill yourself and decided that maybe Dad chose the best option, and that gassing yourself was the easiest way of all.

the wind under the door

One day I came back home to find our tenants in the front room, circling Mum, furiously shouting at her. They were accusing her of overcharging them for their share of the bills. Mum had her arms wrapped tightly around herself, and looked defiant, but I could tell she was on the brink of crying, or screaming. I wondered if I should phone the police, or even the Samaritans. In the end, I phoned my brother.

Rob answered and I tried to explain what was happening. I knew there was nothing he could do from London and that it was impossible for him to swoop in and solve anything, but I badly wanted him to. I held the phone in the direction of the lounge so that Rob could hear the mutiny.

'Put her on the phone,' Rob said.

I plucked Mum from the circle of irate lodgers and dragged her into the hallway. I jammed the receiver to her ear and watched her becoming calmer. Whatever Rob was saying seemed to work.

None of the tenants talked to Mum after the fight. They withheld their rents, took her to county court for what she owed them and moved out when it suited them, but at least I got my bedroom back.

*

Rob visited. He had left his model girlfriend and had a new, shorter one with him called Lori. She gave Mum hyacinths and told her they were 'a sign of rebirth', which we thought was a very London thing to say. She had black hair cut like Louise Brooks, exquisite make-up, a sunny disposition and said 'bolshie' a lot, even though she didn't seem to be very bolshie herself. Lori, who came from a well-off family that had made money in old-time Hollywood, seemed to me to have stepped straight out of the pages of *The Great Gatsby* and into our front room. She said her dad kept offering her an allowance but she turned it down because she valued her independence, which impressed me. She had a Scrabble set with her and we settled down to play a game while Mum was in the kitchen cooking baked potatoes and pizza. It was like we were a proper family and I wanted to hug her for bringing us all together and encouraging us to play games.

'I'm winning yer,' I said to Rob.

'No, you're *beating* me,' he corrected.

'Yeah, that's right,' I said, making a note of the difference.

*

I handed Mum the stiff, blue envelope I had been examining. She held it at a distance and squinted at the postmark, before finally ripping it open and unfolding a single sheet of paper. Her eyes scanned the page.

'She died, she went and died, and he never even told me,' she said.

'Who? Who died?'

'I sent her a birthday card and our address.'

'Who, Mum? Please. Who?'

'I thought it was time to get in touch.'

The letter fluttered from Mum's grip. I snatched it up and read it. Dad's sister had died, my Auntie Vera. Vera's husband had written to tell Mum that she had passed away from cancer six months before.

'He could have told me when it happened,' Mum said.

'He didn't know where we lived.'

'Oh, for God's sake, stop being so reasonable. It wouldn't have been hard to find out where we were. Other people have, especially when they're after money.'

My dad's sister was dead. None of Dad's family were left now. His father had died and his mother, and now his sister.

Vera had spoken with the same Kentish accent as Dad and now she was gone. Mum's sister-in-law had died. Undoing the past was out of reach. Mum had left it too long. We had not seen Vera since Dad had died, as though his death had churned up so much blame nobody could meet again. I often blamed myself for what he did, so I imagine everybody had done something or not done something that they regretted and considered might have saved him. I would never forget the kiss I avoided him giving me, even though I tried not to linger over the memory.

Mum was crying over Vera, so I went to make her a cup of tea. I put the kettle on and thought of knocks on doors and letters arriving out of the blue. It made me never want to read another letter or open another front door again.

*

The bank repossessed the house.

In the lounge, I looked out of the bay window and said goodbye to the main road, the same road my dad had driven me along the final time I saw him. I remembered how Frank, the guest who had sex in the back room with our neighbour Rita, had described it as the spine of England. And so I thought of it now as the central part of a body that was soon to disappear from my life.

A song came to me, or at least part of one. It drummed away in my head. It had been a verse I'd learnt in junior school. Our second year class teacher Mr Ramsbottom believed in hanging and thought tramps were despicable because they didn't pay taxes. He gave me a speech to learn on the Colt 45, part of a school assembly he prepared for our class to deliver on guns, though I never performed it. He told us, with an angry punch of his fist in the air, that the headmaster had asked him to change the subject, so we had to do it on cars instead. Afterwards, I remember standing on the stage with a group of us singing:

'Oh you'll never get to heaven
(Oh you'll never get to heaven)
In an old Ford car
(In an old Ford car)
'Cause an old Ford car
('Cause an old Ford car)
Won't get that far
(Won't get that far)'

That was the song playing in my head, as though it was the soundtrack to my life. I stared at the dark grey dust that striped the entire outside of the window. I realised it was probably from the smoke that blew out from exhaust pipes, and I thought about the invisible stain of carbon monoxide.

Far from being upset about losing the house, Mum was flushed with excitement at the prospect of moving again. She stood next to me in the living room, rubbing her hands together and smiling.

'We're seven miles out,' she said.

'From what?' I asked.

'Seven miles out from where we're going of course,' she replied.

It didn't seem much of a distance.

*

We moved to a red-bricked terraced house in Rusholme that Mum had bought at a bargain price, managing to get a mortgage despite our last house being possessed. She didn't explain the details, but I imagined that Rob must have helped her out with the deposit the bank required.

We unpacked our cardboard boxes, straightened out our possessions and realised that we owned a lot of continental quilts. We got the telly working and sat down on the settee to watch, both of us wrapped in a quilt, as we didn't have any gas yet. The nearby road was lined with curry restaurants and sari shops, and Mum called it 'Little Bombay' and soon developed a taste for onion bhajis.

brynn

She had kept the letter, for some reason, and once they had unpacked the boxes in the house, she read it again, alone in her bedroom. She looks at the letter and wonders what it all means. Ronald had been too young to die, and now his sister was dead at fifty.

> *Dear Brynn,*
>
> *Thank you very much for Vera's birthday card but I just thought I should let you know that Vera passed away of pancreatic cancer six months ago. She died as peacefully as possible. I hope life is treating you and the kids well.*
>
> *Love from,*
>
> *Jim*

She decides there is no real point in keeping the letter. She'll never write to Jim again, or see him again. He means nothing to her. She thinks of Vera, of the time she first met her, and how she had felt the bite of her disapproval. But now Vera is well and truly dead, and why did she even care what Vera thought of her in the first place – or anyone else for that matter? She realises with a jolt that she no longer gives a damn about what anyone thinks of her. She is free. She rips the letter up into tiny pieces and drops it from a height, watching with satisfaction as it flutters to the carpet like snow.

walk the street

'I forgot,' Mum said.

'Mrs Westbourne, if I had your debts it would be like a nail in my coffin. I could never forget!'

Mum began to cry and I glared at the man in the suit, with his precisely-cut, fine, grey hair, who looked like I imagined an undertaker would look. I'd opened the door to leave the house one afternoon and found him standing outside. In a flash he was through the door and in the lounge with Mum, provoking misery. He stuttered at her in anger, demanding an explanation for her moonlight flit and the whereabouts of the money she owed to the Co-op. I thought of all the things Mum had got on the 'never-never' from the Co-op for the boarding house, including all the bedding, and wondered exactly how much she owed.

She pushed him away and he resisted, his hands flapping, so she kept pushing.

'Hands off, Mrs Westbourne, hands off.'

'Get out, you awful little man.'

'This will not be the last you hear from us,' he said before Mum slammed the door on him.

A tight, invisible band strangled my brain. I fled to my bedroom and lay down and fretted. I had begun to paint the wall red and the dark, wooden wardrobe white but had never finished and they stared accusingly at me, so I closed my eyes.

'What'll happen now?' I asked Mum later.

'Oh, it'll sort itself out, these things do. It'll go to county court and they'll order me to pay off a pound a month of what I owe. It'll take them years to get their money!' she said, triumphantly. She sipped on her tea and gasped, a sound of enjoyment which annoyed me, but then I felt mean that it did. Why did I have to get so worked up over a simple sound?

The days that Mum and I had no market research to do we stayed in bed till late. One day we didn't get up till four o'clock in the afternoon. A day wiped out was a good thing in my eyes. Our gas was cut off as our bills went unpaid, so when we did get up we sat on the settee wrapped in quilts and watched telly and drank tea for as long as we had coins for the electric meter.

*

On my seventeenth birthday I got out of bed and went and crouched in the airing cupboard between the slatted, pale pine shelves. I shut the door and wallowed in the darkness.

According to the girl in the playground at primary school all those years ago, seventeen was the age you apparently discovered if you had schizophrenia. I had a feeling of foreboding. It was creeping up on me. I was going to get it. I had told Mum about a dream where I'd floated out of my body and had twirled around in the air and looked down at myself in bed. She had told me it was the kind of dream schizophrenics got.

I needed to get away before the voices began.

*

Nolly was someone I tried to kiss the first time that I met her at the Manchester Musicians Collective. She wasn't interested in kissing me, but we saw each other around at gigs and became friendly. After she left to begin her degree at Oxford, I was impressed with myself that I knew someone studying at such a place. Nolly would return to Manchester in her holidays and she would seek me out at the Haçienda. One summer night we were in the toilets daubing our names in red lipstick on the mirror when the subject of India came up.

'I want to go next Christmas but no one'll come with me,' Nolly said.

'I'll come,' I said. I could tell she didn't believe me.

I had thought that Paris might be the first place I ever visited abroad, but India was good enough. I sent Nolly a letter to let her know I meant it. She wrote back to me and it became real. India was on the horizon. I had six months to get the cash together, so I began to save up. There was nothing like living with a plan, I realised.

'I don't know why you're bothering,' Mum said. 'It's practically like living in India round here anyway.'

'Travel broadens the mind,' I said, immediately regretting my choice of cliché as she gave a disparaging smile.

As well as getting her shopping 'on tick' from the corner shop, Mum frequently used a moneylender, who came directly to the house. She called him the 'Carpet Man' for some reason and was quite fond of his charming smile. His interest rates were high, and soon she began to have to borrow money from him just to pay him off what she owed him in interest. She came to me for a loan instead. I agreed to lend her some of my savings for India because she said it wouldn't be for long. But on the day I needed to give money to Nolly, who had bought our plane tickets with her own money, Mum began to act evasive.

'I need the money for Nolly!' I yelled. 'She'll think I'm messing her around.'

'I don't know about that,' said Mum. 'I don't have it.'

'You owe it me!'

'In fact,' said Mum, stirring my anger, 'you're not having it back. It's rent.'

'But yer weren't charging me any,' I said. 'Yer never asked for any.'

'You should have thought to pay some.'

'Yer should have said!'

Mum stood up. She crossed her arms against the bulging darts of her dress.

'Come on, Mum, please!'

'I'm putting my foot down with a firm hand, that's what I'm doing, and it's about time.'

'But yer promised you'd give it me back.'

'Well, I haven't got it, so there.'

'I just want the fuckin' money!'

'Don't you go using language like that with me, madam.'

'Give me my fuckin' money!'

'And if you think I'm going to sign your passport you've got another thing coming. You're under eighteen and you won't be getting a passport if I don't sign that form.'

'Then I'll fake yer signature.'

'Oh no you won't. I'll report you to the Government and you'll never be able to go anywhere ever again.'

'Don't think I'm going looking after you when you're old, yer bitch!'

Mum grabbed her shoe from her foot, and launched herself at me.

'I wish you'd never been born!' she screamed.

There was a ferocious, animal energy to her as she slapped the leather sole of her shoe against my face, one side and then the other, over and over until I sank into a huddle, my arms shielding my face. She was officially mad. This proved it. Mum hit my arms but the fight in her had gone. She stopped and began to laugh.

I had blood in my mouth, yet all Mum could do was laugh like a maniac. I got out of the house. I ran and passed houses that flickered with televisions and life. I licked the thick, metallic taste from my lips. I wished I had never been born. If only I had never set foot in this stupid world. What was the point of going on? It was only going to get worse. I wanted to run into the path of a juggernaut so I could wake up in intensive care and find my body in the same state as my mind. Then everybody would realise just how fucked up I was. Or maybe it would be best never to wake up at all.

Dad had not stayed around to watch me grow up because he knew what I'd grow up to become. A slag, a good-for-nothing, everything he would have despised, and I was always having a go at Mum in my head because she had no friends, but did I really have any friends? There was Tranny Andy, who was saving up for a face lift even though he was only nineteen, and there was Harry, with his long, painted fingernails and his guitars who thought I was a virgin, and there was Nolly, oh and there were others that I saw, but were they proper friends? Were they friends like other people had friends? How would I know? I never talked to anyone about anything real. Was I even real? Had Dad ever been really real?

All the years I'd thought of Dad, all the years he'd run through my life like a fault line, my brain, my heart (if it existed), my soul (if it existed), colonised by him, ready to split me open at any time, yet how many memories of him did I have?

Here was one. The colour TV being delivered and I'm on my own with Dad and excited and it feels like the start of something good, and he turns the television on and it comes to life, and later he lets me stay up late and we're sitting down watching *Within These Walls*.

Two. Going to see *Bugsy Malone* with Dad and asking if I could lie down in the aisle of the cinema to watch the film and being surprised when he said that I could.

Three. Spilling Vimto on the carpet and being glad that Dad didn't notice and sitting on the wet patch all night hoping it would disappear. It did.

Four. Dad taking the stabilisers off my bike and watching me as I pedalled along the pavement without falling off.

Five. Seeing Dad spray-painting my second-hand bike blue. Manchester City blue.

Six. Shouting for Dad when the bogeyman was looking at me through the toilet window and being relieved when he rescued me.

Seven. Going with Dad to Comet to buy a hairdryer and a steel watch for Mum's birthday.

Eight. Being in a toy shop with Dad as he bought me a Meccano set for Christmas, and him asking me if I was sure it was what I really wanted, as there would be no surprises on Christmas day.

Nine. The time he picked me up from school in his old, bronze car, the car that he owned before the salesman car.

Ten. Being at home with him on my own and slipping off his shoes and tickling his feet and Dad tickling mine and feeling happy as I ran off with his shoe to hide it behind the landing curtain and him finally getting annoyed and wanting his shoe back: his slip-on, black shoe.

Eleven. Saying to him, 'Excuse me, please may I leave the table?' I must have said it a lot of times, but it was as though it had become one single memory.

Twelve. Dad smacking me because I wouldn't go to bed.

Thirteen. Doing my homework, where I had to make a list of different kinds of measuring devices and Dad suggesting Intelligence Quota.

Fourteen. Dad taking me to his office Christmas party, where I met Father Christmas, who I was still young enough to believe in.

Fifteen. Seeing Dad kissing Mum in the hallway and Mum looking happy.

Sixteen. Showing Dad my broken front tooth when he turned up after one of his disappearing trips. He didn't say anything, he just smiled.

Seventeen. After the last disappearing trip Dad took before he died, seeing him sitting very still on a dining-room chair in the kitchen and looking sad.

Eighteen. Dad driving just me to Lyme Park, but it was raining when we got there, so we never got out of the car and he drove us back home straight away.

Nineteen. Dad falling into the river and getting his trousers soaked and looking embarrassed.

Twenty. Dad teaching me to hold a ping-pong bat.

Twenty-one. Dad teaching me cards and the card trick.

Twenty-two. Dad showing me how to make an origami bird.

Twenty-three. Dad hitting my sister because he caught her eating a bowl of cornflakes after school.

Twenty-four. Dad on Margate beach building a car out of sand.

Twenty-five. Dad hanging his jacket on the side of the armchair, the pockets rattling with change.

Twenty-six. Dad spreading a Weetabix with Stork margarine.

Twenty-seven. Dad shouting at me when he found me opening my birthday present, a box of Milk Tray, in the middle of the night, before he realised I must have been sleepwalking.

Twenty-eight. The time Dad was doing the crossword puzzle and he said I got a clue right.

Twenty-nine. The day after I had my tonsils out, Dad visiting the hospital and giving me a colouring book.

Thirty. Dad looking happy after a shopping trip with Mum.

Thirty-one. Dad letting me read to him from an Enid Blyton book when I was sick and off school.

Thirty-two. Dad telling me he liked my bedroom after I'd made it really tidy, even though Mum was worried it was too neat for a child.

Thirty-three. Dad letting me eat pie and chips out of the newspaper in his bronze car.

Thirty-four. Dad saying that if I was quiet for half an hour he'd give me a pound. I didn't talk or make a noise and when the time was up he put an ornament from the mantelpiece into my hands and said, 'There you go, that weighs about a pound.'

Thirty-five. Dad taking me to see Manchester City play.

Thirty-six. The very last time I saw Dad in his new car.

Had I left any out? Maybe. But I couldn't think of any more. Thirty-six memories: the results of eleven years of knowing him. Averaging out at about three memories a year; there must be more. Where did things go? Where did life go? Where did my dad's life go? Why didn't I give Dad a reason to live? Wasn't that the point of why people had children?

I gave up running. I had no idea where I was any more. It was late. The streets were deserted. The pubs were shut and the roads were empty. Everything seemed useless, even running away, so I turned around and began to head home. Even though it was the last place I wanted to be, I didn't know what else to do. I would work out a way to kill myself later.

Footsteps were approaching from behind and I saw him out of the corner of my eye, the man, but I didn't look directly at him. My first reaction was to run but I didn't want to seem scared. I began to find it harder to breathe and my throat was getting smaller and I kept gulping, painful gulps of air, but I did my best to hide it from him.

'Why aren't you frightened of me?' he asked, eventually.

'Because I've got a black belt in karate,' I said.

'Yer joking?'

'No.'

I tried to walk like a karate expert would, though I was at a loss as to what that would be like.

'Yer tits are massive,' he said. 'They are, aren't they? They're dead big.'

I managed a sly sideways glance and saw that his cock was out of his jeans and in his hand. He's going to rape me, I thought. He may even murder me. I was going to wind up as another column inch in the newspaper. He stepped in front of me and leered. Was this the beginning of the end?

And in that moment, I realised that no matter how much I hated myself, I wanted to survive. All I thought about was being worthless and dying, and yet I wanted to carry on. It seemed so ridiculous. I almost laughed, but thought better of it when I felt his breath and the smell of danger.

How was I going to get away from him?

And then it came to me. I would ask him out. So I did.

'What did yer say?' he said.

I stopped and looked directly into his wild eyes.

'So do yer want to meet up or what?' I said. I pointed to a nearby pub. 'Let's meet there at seven-thirty tomorrow.'

'Honest?' he said.

'Yeah. But on one condition – yer not to go following me home. I want to get to know yer first.'

'Yer not having me on?'

'Why would I go and do that?'

His face cracked into a warped smile. I heard the coarse grate of his zip closing.

'See yer tomorrow,' I said, waving my shaking hand with fake enthusiasm.

He shuffled away, still looking over his shoulder and watching me. I thought of him in that pub the next day, waiting. I headed home, the safest place for me.

I didn't have keys so I had to knock my mum out of bed. Behind the bubbled glass of the front door I could see her descending the stairs, like a growing candyfloss in her pink dressing gown. I was dreading what would erupt when she opened the door.

But when she did, her face was softer and I knew she'd been crying.

'You'll get your money. I'll get it from the Carpet Man,' she said. 'And I'm sorry I snapped at you earlier.'

'That's okay, Mum,' I told her. 'Everything'll be all right.'

where the sun beats

I clutched my arms around Nolly's waist as her moped veered and bumped over the roads leading us out of Manchester. We arrived in the village and Nolly turned off the engine with a final stutter and we walked the scooter to a free space and kicked the stand down.

Stiffening ourselves against the wind that had suddenly whipped into place, we trudged arm in arm past the cottages that quaintly lined the streets and along the paved path. We walked by the ancient church and then we were there, in the graveyard I had for so long wanted to visit.

I had thought that the cemetery would be peaceful, a place of rest, but the flat land was full of bony, naked trees and tall, yellow grasses that bent with aching violent protest against the wind, as though they were waving at me. The winter sun struck the white crosses and made them glow; they dotted the cemetery like punctuation marks.

I left Nolly so I could search on my own for the grave. I leant over, deciphering names, dates, inscriptions, occasionally touching the surface of the stone. We are all going to die, I thought. I realised just how little death is talked about, seeing as it comes to us all. Then I thought of how in the course of history I was inconsequential. I was nothing at all. All these feelings, what did they really matter? They were nothing. In a hundred years I would be gone from the earth. Dad and I would be even.

It was then that I found her grave. Sylvia Plath Hughes. Placed on it were a few smeary jam jars of wilting flowers in murky water and a cellophane-wrapped, rotting bouquet. I wondered if the flowers were from the son and daughter she had left behind. How often did they come here? I wished that Dad had been put somewhere that I knew about so I could visit him and lay flowers on his grave.

Dad and Sylvia were both killed by gas. Dad in his car and Sylvia with her head in her oven. What was gassing yourself like? Was it like drifting into a velvet sleep? I hoped so. I wished that Dad was buried here in Heptonstall in windy Yorkshire, close to Sylvia, who would surely understand him.

What had Dad left behind? A widow, three children, a mother and a sister who were now both dead. If Dad had any friends then I didn't know about them. They had never come forward to tell me anything about him. He had left so little for me to figure him out by. At least Sylvia's children had her poetry. All I had were a few fading photographs. I wanted a flick book, a movie. I wanted to discover a mountain of evidence that he had existed. Even the ashes would do.

Leaving Sylvia, I made my way to the far edge of the graveyard. Beyond it was a flat field. Or was it a moor? I was frustrated that I was unable to name the land, the trees and all the details that were around me. If only I had the names I could be more precise. If only I could find all the words that applied to Dad, he would come back to me, if only in my mind.

Bright, dancing stars appeared and a rising blackness began to eclipse my vision. Mum had told me that Dad had blackouts. Was this what was happening? A sharp turn of my head snapped me back to consciousness and that was the moment I realised what Dad had left me, and what my inheritance truly was. Dad wasn't walking beside me – he was buried inside of me. He was never going to go away. He was never going to leave me. In the shadows of the graves, I knew that whatever darkness he had felt I felt too. That was our connection and it always would be.

And that is when it happened. I stroked my face and there they were. I wiped them away across my cheek but they kept on coming. I licked them from my lips and tasted their salt. It seemed as though I was melting and thawing. All around me the natural world was protesting, and so was I, and I couldn't stop. I did not want to stop. I kept on crying until my howls, drowned out by the wind, subsided and stopped.

I made my way back to Nolly.

'Good grief,' she said at the sight of me, my mascara probably smudged across my face. I couldn't help laughing.

As I wiped under my eyes with my fingertips, Nolly announced that perhaps it was a good time to go and find a café that served a proper cream tea.

*

That night I dreamed of Dad. In the dream I thought to myself that I had been waiting years to see him, and it was finally happening.

I was sitting at Grandma Westbourne's table. She was busy at her sewing machine. Dad was sitting sideways on my lap, and he wore a long, white robe. I was surprised he wasn't wearing his suit, and thought it was a bit clichéd that he was wearing white but, even so, I was glad that his robe must mean he was an angel. I took in his profile and somehow knew that he was unable to speak so I said nothing to him. Dad sat there on my knee, and I could feel the real weight of him and I knew, I really knew, that he was there.

*

Mum bought a car on hire purchase and became the giddy owner of a blue Mini Clubman. When she picked up the car from the lot she said the salesman had to remind her what the foot pedals were for, she hadn't driven for so long. We took the car for a ride and Mum drove aimlessly around the streets, excited by the prospect of having wheels.

'Your dad taught me to drive. He couldn't believe it when I passed, he didn't think I had it in me. One time there were police sirens and he thought they were after me because I was a bit all over the place when I was learning. We never had so many arguments as when he was teaching me to drive.'

She turned the corner and I tried to ask a question about Dad. Why, after all these years, did I find it so difficult? A voice inside of me told me to ask away. One of the things I had never asked, but had always wanted to know, was where he was cremated and if there was a headstone or a plaque, but I couldn't bring myself to do it – as though to talk about Dad diminished him, made him too everyday.

'You're a really good driver, Mum,' I said, instead.

'You know, I'd really gone and forgotten how much I enjoyed it.'

She smiled and pressed a little harder on the accelerator.

I thought of my brother and sister, who had got on with their lives, and wondered if they'd asked questions without me knowing – maybe they had enough answers. Rob had formed a record company in London. Susan was still, miraculously in my eyes, going out with Greg, the same boyfriend that Dad had known. They had moved to London and she had got a job as a dresser in a major theatre, the start of great things, according to Greg. Their lives had taken shape.

Mum started a diet and began to study the lonely-heart columns of the *Manchester Evening News*. Together we tried to read between the lines of the brief descriptions and figure out what the men were really like.

'Sunlight and the Black Sea are both medically proven to help psoriasis. Maybe one day I'll make it there,' Mum said, as she unpacked her old sun lamp.

'Where is the Black Sea?' I asked her.

'Oh, I don't know, some place abroad,' she said. 'Somewhere foreign.'

She sat in front of the small, conical lamp, exposing various parts of her skin for ten minutes at a time. Dust whorls floated into the air as the orange light landed onto Mum's blemished skin. She hadn't used the lamp since Dad died. As I watched her, odd and alien in her tight, elastic, green goggles, attempting to get rid of those red, raised patches, with their silvery, white scales, I felt guilty that I had always hated her psoriasis, as though she had deliberately made it an extension of herself.

One evening Mum and Maureen from next door went to the pub, where Mum met the man whose lonely hearts advert she had replied to. According to Mum, the man had become drunk and maudlin and had cried. She and Maureen couldn't stop laughing as they recounted the story of taking the man home and pulling his boots off and putting him to bed. 'It was a right palaver,' Maureen said.

'My husband was the only man I've ever been with,' I overheard Mum tell Maureen, who insisted that Mum should keep on looking for a man, as she was only forty-five and had years ahead of her.

The maudlin-man experience didn't stop Mum. I was relieved as she circled other lonely hearts with her red Biro. 'I might even put my own advertisement in, one of these days,' she said.

*

The airport is a bewildering affair. I would never have known which queue to stand in if it wasn't for Nolly, who has done all this before. She can't believe that I'm off to India and that I've never had a curry. An image of Mum devouring those greasy onion bhajis that she said played havoc with her diet settles in my mind. I watch the thin air hostesses as they pass smartly by on their sharp heels and think about Dad's mistress and wonder what happened to her.

I look around at all the families and wonder what ever happened to my childish idea of studying other people's fathers. Had I ever really got anywhere? It seemed that no dad was the same. I didn't know anyone with the ideal father, they just didn't seem to exist – nor did mothers for that matter. But all the fathers I'd met seemed absent, in one way or another – more so than mothers, which seemed to make sense. I think of all the mad fathers and violent fathers and unfaithful fathers and silent fathers and flirtatious fathers and kind fathers and cowardly fathers that I've met and I know for sure that Dad was the best one of them all.

Nolly mentions that we're flying east but I'm not really sure whether she means the Middle or the Far East. She says that I can look at her guidebook on the flight. I like the idea of finding out everything in the air – between two worlds.

I buckle my seatbelt and look out of the window. Nolly has given me the window seat. As the aircraft taxis onto the runway the drone of the engine fills the cabin. I imagine that all the passengers are thinking about what they are leaving behind.

*

Out of the glove compartment you take the Basildon Bond writing paper and lean the pad against the steering wheel. You explain as clearly as you can your reasons. Under no circumstances do you want your wife to think your decision has anything to do with her.

You finish the letter and fold it neatly in half and put it in the envelope, sliding your tongue along the bitter seal. You address the envelope to your wife and place the letter on the dashboard where the person that will find you will clearly see it. At least it will be a stranger finding you – though a pang of guilt passes through you for the inconvenience you will have caused.

How methodical and organised you are as you attach the length of hose firmly to the exhaust pipe and push it in through the slightly wound-down back passenger window. It is as though all your life has been heading towards this moment. It seems more real than anything you have ever experienced. You fill in the gap between the car frame and window with bunched-up newspaper. You don't want any gas escaping. Nothing should go wrong this time.

You step into the car, settle onto your seat, pull the door shut and turn on the car engine. You are not sure how long it will take, this journey, but you have taken the precaution of filling the tank with petrol so you will get where you want to. You feel a pang that this car doesn't really belong to you, but feel better when you think that the company will get it back soon enough, in much the same condition as you were given it; only a few extra miles on the clock.

You see caught in the passenger seatbelt a few strands of Ann's long brown hair. She is better off without you. They all are. Brynn, Rob, Susan, Ann. You hope that they will understand it was the right thing to do. You would only end up being a burden to them.

Working backwards, rewinding time, thinking of your father and you still feel the weight of his letter in your hand, begging to see you and you still feel the blow at the discovery that he had never been far away at all. Your mother, you have always blamed her for that, but you have done nothing but disappoint her and this is just more of the same. You see Vera, your sister, as a child again, laughing, pulling you out of the fireplace after you'd fallen, backside landing onto hot coals. She's pulling you out, but it's no use. This is all you can do.

The air is filled with the gas and you are going, going to that place, the other side, to the relief of nothing, the best that you could hope for.

Fragments of your time as a wartime evacuee, a train ride, a man leaning over you, flashes of pain and then back home again, swimming in the Margate sea, dappled sunlight, sand between your toes, a table tennis paddle in your hand and you are pushing, spinning, chopping a ping-pong ball back and to, backhand, forehand, darting about, fine footwork, serving that hollow white celluloid ball, slamming it back to your opponent, the Chinese-looking chap who insisted he wasn't Chinese at all, a rally of strength, opposing forces, no dead balls, energy in your lungs, the sound of the clear clicking bounce on the table, your wooden handle gripped confidently in your hand like a firm handshake, an extension of you, the red rubber-coated bat as it hits, the glorious sound of the killer smash as it confounds him, you are winning, you are up, the game is on your side. The motion, the excitement, the quick wit, the rush of energy and being presented with that golden trophy declaring you the Junior Table Tennis Champion of Kent and thinking, if only Dad could see me now, if only he could see me now.

*

Nolly says, 'Here we go.'

We lift off from the runway.

I look down at the houses, the trees, the fields, the motorways, the roads, the streets, the cars – everything turning into a toy town. All the lives being lived below – happy, sad, indifferent – and all the families trying to get by, and the higher the aeroplane gets the less important everything seems to become, with the solid knowledge that it is possible to escape and to rise above it all.

I press my nose against the window and take in what I have only ever seen before on television. We are amongst cloud, fluffy and soft and white, like my childhood idea of heaven. I realise how rarely I look at the sky, at all the air and vapour that surrounds us. In India I will turn eighteen, the key to the door. Independence. Freedom. My life may start to happen and I will begin to live.

It is nearly seven years since Dad died. I read somewhere that every seven years our cells renew themselves and I wonder what cells I have that remain from his time. I can feel the insides of my body shift and reform as we begin to level out above the clouds into the clear blue sky.

· THE LAND BEYOND ·

I read on the internet that every thirty seconds someone, somewhere in the world, kills themselves. My dad never lived long enough to experience the world of the internet, of smart phones and social media, to know a time where the word 'depression' is common currency, though often used superficially to describe a transitory unhappy mood. Perhaps if he was still around he would have found a world that still finds it difficult to talk substantially about mental illness, but that does at least acknowledge that it widely exists.

I realise now that my teenage concerns that Dad was in limbo after he died were beside the point. It was the people he left behind who were in limbo. I can only imagine the conversation I would have had with my mum, Brynn, about him. She died from a stroke five years ago and I never did find a time that felt right to talk to her about my dad.

A couple of years before she died, she pointed to the framed black and white Japanese print of a horse, which had become her joke of the only inheritance we had to fight over after she died, and told me that she remembered buying it on the Isle of Wight with my dad. It was an opening, an opportunity to ask her some things, but, just like all the other possible moments that had come about over the decades, I felt my chest restricting, my throat automatically closing and my mouth drying out. It was as though to talk about Dad not only diminished him, but would release something in me that I didn't want anyone to see or hear. There was one time, though, when I did speak about Dad. Rob was writing a book and he interviewed me about him. As I spoke into the tape recorder, I felt as though I was part of a controlled situation and so the occasion didn't overwhelm me, but, outside of that, I have continued to find it difficult to talk about Dad to any family members.

The trip to India with Nolly took place over thirty years ago and, while the travel book she brought along with her described the culture shock we would experience there, I felt a lessening of shock as I moved away from Stockport. From India onwards, I looked forward to all the departures that there would be in the future. I kept waiting to arrive, for something significant to happen. At twenty-three I was living in London, working as a shop assistant in a health food shop. I had spent years doing various jobs or no job at all, working as a tea girl, a cleaner, signing on the dole, constantly moving around and looking for something to do. Working in the shop, I decided that I was too old to reinvent myself any further and that my chances were over of arriving anywhere where I would find some kind of true purpose. It was around this time I saw an advert for courses at a college in East London. I enrolled in A-level night classes in Photography and Film, and a part-time day course in Video.

College was an opportunity to watch films and to learn to write essays and to take photographs and make videos. While I had chosen to go to college more out of desperation than desire, I soon found that this ability to freeze, slow down and re-examine time felt like an extraordinarily powerful gift. It was here I met an inspirational teacher, who gave me such a love of film that she changed my life. Discussing films and making films and videos gave me a true purpose, and was something I wanted to pursue like nothing else.

I applied to Central Saint Martins College of Art and Design to study Fine Art, Film and Video. Steeped in angst about what to wear to the interview, my flatmate stole a hat for me. It was a red corduroy flat cap, with daisies along the brim, and she put it on my head at an angle and decided I looked suitably art school material. At the interview panel I presented the videos and photographs I had made and one of the lecturers asked me what else I had been doing since I had left school. I felt embarrassed by my lack of achievements but mentioned India and that I had kept a journal, trying to think of ways I could impress on her that I was interesting and worthy of a place at such a prestigious art school, even though I couldn't draw that well, or felt in any way like an artist.

Getting the letter telling me I had been awarded a place melted my recent disjointed past away and the thought of three years ahead, filled with things to do, felt like luxury. It was 1990, the time of grants and fees being paid, the hint of student loans being introduced only towards the end of my degree. Throughout the course, I carried on working at the health food shop on Saturdays and in the holidays. I felt anchored, no longer adrift. Life was stable.

In the first week at Central Saint Martins we made a video self-portrait. I used the few photographs I had of my dad in a

wordless, abstract piece, which never explained who he was or why
I was showing the photographs. It just felt the right thing to do, that
my identity would always be tied up with his. I returned to my dad
for my degree show film. It was a reconstruction of the last day I
saw him – his hands on the steering wheel, his car vanishing into
the distance.

Brynn never saw my degree film. When we had our final year
show at the cinema at BAFTA, I sent her an invite, not imagining
she would make the trip, but wanting her to know about it. When
I arrived on the day of the show, the person on the front desk asked
if I was Ann and gave me a message from my mum that she was
sorry but was unable to come. It made me smile to think of Brynn's
thought process in phoning up BAFTA and describing me to the
person on the other end of the telephone, rather than phoning me
and telling me she wasn't coming. My sister came though and just
before my film came on screen I said to Susan, 'It's about Dad.'
Afterwards we never mentioned the film or Dad again.

When I told Brynn I had graduated with a first-class honours
degree, she suggested we should take out an advertisement in the
Stockport Advertiser to 'show that silly school you were never daft.'
By this point, Brynn had met a man she would spend the rest of her
life with, not through a classified advert, but in a pub. She gave him
the name Bobby, because she didn't like the one he'd been given
at birth – Oswalt. In some ways I always thought of Bobby as her
invention. The only similarity to Dad was that he enjoyed crossword puzzles, but really he was as unlike Dad as it was possible to
be. He had the word 'kiss' tattooed on his inner lip and 'love' and
'hate' inked on his knuckles. Mum hinted proudly that he had been
in prison, though this was never verified. When I first met him,

Brynn was disappointed that I wouldn't smoke his dope with him, something she took up briefly with gusto.

At Brynn's funeral, Bobby turned up wailing, in jeans, clutching twenty-four red roses. While Dad seemed to be the image of a 1950's refined matinée idol, Bobby always reminded me of Oliver Reed in beard-and-drink mode. I think my mum loved him because he didn't care about any social niceties. He would flick his roll-up ash on the carpet and drive without a driving licence and knock down walls in the places they lived without consulting the landlord. Once my mum phoned me to tell me that she and Bobby had been arrested for criminal damage, and her voice was filled with rebellious excitement as she told me how she'd resisted having her fingerprints taken at the police station and been put in a cell.

Brynn moved a lot over the years. Her life's work was buying *The Lady* and looking at the classifieds. Here she would find a house or flat to let, usually owned by an aristocrat, who would rent it out in return for a small sum and some babysitting. She presented herself as a widow, and never told them about Bobby, who would covertly come to live with her. She lived in a few places like this, as well as squatting a flat in Eastbourne at one point and living in a car for a few weeks. She remained a wanderer, always looking for something elusive that she tied up with being in the right house, the right flat, the right area, which she never seemed to find. On her sixtieth birthday she revealed that what she had always wanted to be was a bag lady.

My mum's first stroke, before the one that would kill her, took her to a ward in Rhyl Hospital in North Wales. I visited her, got out of the train station and walked by the shut-down shops and pubs to the nearby hospital. She woke up from a deep sleep, her speech slurred, and said, 'Well, I'll never be able to say double-barrelled names again now.' She dozed again and I looked out of the ward window, at the fine landscape that surrounded a town that looked like it had been torn apart and forgotten, and I thought about her constant need to move, to find something that was always out of reach. When Brynn woke up again she looked at me kindly and said, 'When I'm in heaven, will you be all right without me?' I realised by the fond way she said heaven that it was somewhere she was enthusiastically anticipating as her next major move.

Brynn didn't survive the second stroke she had. When she died I experienced a different kind of grief than when Dad had died. My adult experience of parent bereavement seemed easier to cope with. I felt a physical pain that concentrated itself in my chest, and I found I was able to cry, which eased the pain. I realised that when my dad died I was at an age when my life was tied to his in such a significant way it was difficult to unknot the complications after he'd gone. Brynn had lived to her early seventies and I wasn't dependent on her any more for my day-to-day life. I never did look after her when she got old, as I had threatened her in my teenage argument, so she wasn't dependent on me; we were untied.

After Brynn's death, I had no problem dreaming about her. She seemed to be in my dreams often, sitting drinking a mug of tea, talking about another house move, surrounded by hilly piles of ripped fabric, making the rag rugs she loved to make, but there was one dream I had of her that also featured Dad. It was only the second dream I have ever had that he was in. It felt as precious as a rare celluloid silent film and I tried to preserve it by repeating it constantly in my mind. The dream was similar in look to the Japanese brush strokes of the horse picture that my mum and dad had bought together. Through this black and white landscape, Mum and Dad, young again, walked together, arm in arm, deep in private, unheard, conversation.

I think of film-making as a form of making dreams come to life; of asking questions too difficult to ask in real life; of constructing something meaningful out of messy and difficult experiences. I think back to being the eleven-year-old girl the day the police came to the door to tell us the news about Dad. I'm no longer frozen in that moment. I'm no longer her. But she's part of me, and I know that my father's suicide gave me the desire to truly examine what it is to live, to find a way to try and make sense of the world and to resurrect the lost. It is, without a doubt, why I became a film-maker.

acknowledgments

Thank you to all the following:

Cairo Cannon, Jane Grisewood, Brenda Reid, Joan Scanlon,
Chris Wyatt and Bev Zalcock for being early readers and for their
support and advice.

Louise Lamont and Emily Thomas for the journey into the light.

Jane Burnard and Oliver Holden-Rea for noticing and
Karen Browning for bringing it to notice.

For being there, and here: the Morleys: Paul, Jayne, Madeleine,
Natasha, Florence; to the Mitchells: Sally, Andrew, Sian, Lizzie; and
to Matthew Bates, Jane Cannon, Sara Chambers, Susan Ferguson,
Liane Harris, Dave Haslam, Liz Levy, Polly Leys, James Lobjoit,
Heidi Locher, Kate Norrish, Maxine Peake, Darren Philpott,
Claire Rasul, Zah Rasul, Tony Roche, Luc Roeg, Archie and
Joann Southgate, and Tracey Thorn.